THE INCA CURSE

An Adventure YOU control

Artic Computing's
Adventure B

Adapted for print by

Stephen Harris

OAK TREE BOOKS

The Inca Curse
Published in 2022 by
Oak Tree Books
oaktreebooks.uk

Copyright © 2022 Subvert Limited

Adaptation and additional material by Stephen Harris
Illustrations by Emily Botta
Cover image by Gary Arnott

Artic Computing is a registered
Trademark of Subvert Limited.

An Adventure YOU control

Gamebooks aren't quite the same as traditional books. Here, you play the part of the book's protagonist, and everything is decided by you – the route taken, the treasures plundered, and the foes battled. Your goal is to triumph over or escape from whatever obstacles stand in your way – and hopefully find some treasures to take home in the process.

Sometimes this kind of story is called 'interactive fiction', or 'choose your own adventure' – the latter being a trademark currently owned by Chooseco but originally registered by Bantam Books, publisher of a highly popular series of gamebooks during the 1980s and 1990s.

***

This book is based on the computer game *Adventure B: The Inca Curse*, an extremely popular title published by Artic during the early days of home computing.

Throughout your journey, you will find yourself dodging around deadly traps that have been laying in wait for hapless intruders, battling ancient guardians from an empire long since consigned to history, and uncovering artefacts that have remained hidden in the depths of the Earth for centuries untold – all in pursuit of a treasure spoken of only in myth.

You will also come across a variety of different items that may prove useful to you, be they weapons or gold. A sheet is provided on which you can keep track of your inventory, and you can make copies of if you don't want to write in the book itself. Alternatively, you can buy a book of gamesheets for the whole Artic Computing Adventure series from all good bookshops.

It seems that now you have the knowledge and tools needed to plunder the depths of a temple not touched by human hands for hundreds of years, so you are now ready to face 1981's...

INCA CURSE!

Game Rules

Inventory Management

On your journey, you will come across a wealth of different items, from treasure to weapons, and everything in between. Though you may be tempted to try and stash all you find in your pack, there is only space enough for five items in total. You must be careful choosing what to pick up and what to leave, as you'll need to decide whether you wish to hoard treasure, arm yourself to deal with enemy threats, or try to strike a balance between the two.

Treasure

Your aim in this adventure will be to find as much treasure as possible, escaping the temple with as valuable a haul as you can. Numerous items can be found throughout the temple, each of which is worth a certain amount of points ranging from slight to staggering. Defeated enemies will also drop all kinds of items, from gemstones to golden trinkets most valuable. Beware however, as fighting an enemy to gain such treasures risks your limited health; only *you* can decide whether the risk is worth the reward.

Once you have escaped the temple, turn to the back of the book to determine the value of your items, and add them together. Present your total to the museum curator on the pages afterwards to find out just how brave an adventurer you proved to be. Of course, subsequent runs and alternate paths *may* yield better results – or your untimely demise.

Combat

The temple's many traps will not be your only obstacles throughout this journey. Enemies lurk around every corner, waiting for the chance to strike out at you. Some encounters can be fled from – however, other foes will trap you in a room with them, where the only way past is to beat them in single combat. It is best that you prepare yourself accordingly.

Combat consists of you and your enemy taking turns attempting to reduce the other's Hit Points (HP) to **0**, with you always taking the first turn.

To determine the damage you deal to the enemy that turn, roll a six-sided die. Add to the value rolled any attack modifiers granted by your equipped weapon and reduce the result by your opponent's defence. Subtract this number from your enemy's HP, and end your turn.

The enemy will then attack you. You will be given the enemy's attack score, though if you have defensive equipment, subtract its defence modifier from this score; this is then deducted from your HP.

Starting Items

Your starting HP is **25**. You also begin your journey with a **Medical Kit**, and a **Machete**. The Medical Kit restores your HP to **25** upon use, but can only be used once — it then disappears from your inventory. The **Machete**'s primary function is as a tool, but also provides a small bonus to attack rolls.

Medical Kit: Restores health to full, but takes up one inventory slot.

Machete: A simple blade with a curved head and sharp edge. Useful primarily as an exploration tool, but can also be used as a weapon. **+2** attack modifier.

Adventure B: Inca Curse
Game Sheet

Hit Points

Attack Modifier

Defence Modifier

Item #1

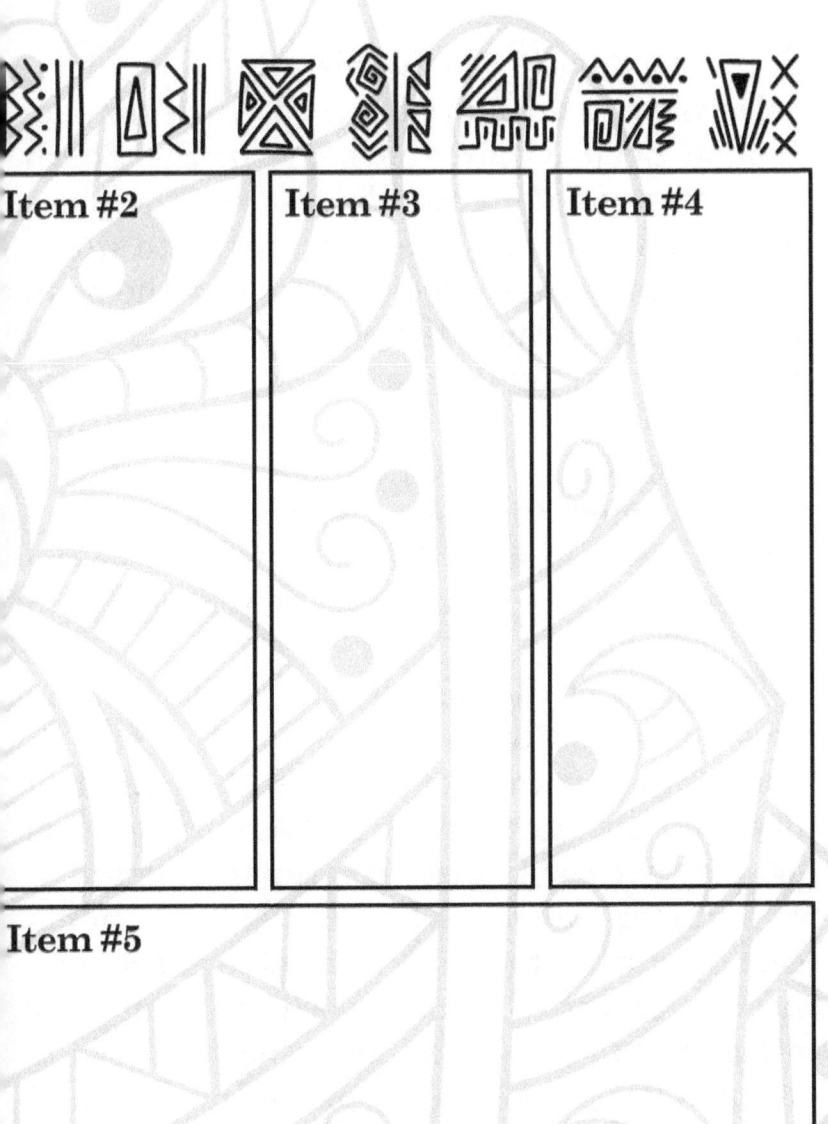

Item #2

Item #3

Item #4

Item #5

Your Adventure Begins...

Since the days of the Spanish Conquistadors, tales have been told of a great Inca temple, hidden deep within the heart of the South American jungle. Legends describe the place as a towering mass of carved bricks and stone, piled so high that it looks as though the peak touches the clouds themselves. Yet despite the historical significance of the architecture and the library's worth of knowledge historians could no doubt glean from such a fine specimen, that is not what drew so many people's attention to the story. No, it was the vast hoards of treasure said to reside within its depths.

The part of the temple that could be seen was rumoured to be but one part of a vast, sprawling network of tunnels that reached deep into the Earth. Each of these tunnels was said to have been lined with traps and guarded by sinister magics – be they enchantments cast on statues to create invincible guardians, necromancy used to raise warriors from their eternal slumber, or arcane objects allowing the holder passage into places most would never be able to tread. All of this was supposed to have been to guard the emperor that called the depths home – as well as his riches.

Metals of every kind, be it common iron or lustrous gold; gems of all shapes and sizes, with the largest among them said to be the size of a man's fist; perfectly-preserved artefacts that any scholar would pay a fortune simply to view... the temple's treasury was said to have held all of these and more, locked behind layer upon layer of stone, earth, and magic.

Of course, few have sought out the temple, believing it to be nothing but the ramblings of superstitious conquerors, or the musings of a bored traveller looking to entertain his companions by the campfire. The few that have followed whatever clues and maps they could uncover always returned empty-handed, finding nothing but dirt for all of their troubles.

You, however, believe that you hold the key to determining once and for all whether the story is fact or fiction.

Verified by numerous accredited scholars as the right age to be a genuine article, the map you recently acquired has led you to a jungle clearing, far from any settlement. By the looks of things, the area has been left untouched by man for centuries, with only the flora and fauna to inhabit it.

And it is in this jungle clearing that your adventure to the heart of the temple begins...

1

Your body is drenched in sweat. Your pack, despite you having done all you could to cut out unnecessary weight, feels heavy on your back after trekking through vast stretches of treacherous terrain. Though your supplies are adequate, and your water canteen full enough that you are in no danger of running out any time soon, you would rather eat your own leg before digging into another tin of whatever reconstituted meat lurks at the bottom of your pack.

Despite all this, you have a mission in mind, and you will not let any obstacle – be it natural or self-imposed – stop you from completing it. You glance at the map to make sure that you are on the right path. It seems that you are, but no matter how much the map may have been restored, there is no escaping the fact that the thing was drawn hundreds of years before you were even born. Routes may have changed, new dangers arisen, or old ones subdued – everything on it will have to be taken with a grain of salt, if it can be believed at all. The first instance of this arises when you come to a fork in the path that was not documented on the map – leaving you to figure out the correct way forward yourself. To the south is a dense thicket of trees, vines, and other assorted foliage. You could potentially cut your way through it, as long as you have something to cut it with. To the west, you see a relatively flat stretch of land with only a few stray branches blocking your path. There is a similar scene to the west, with the only discernible difference being a few large stones resting upon the jungle floor. If you wish to try the south path, turn to **21**. To try going west along the flat route, turn to **14**. To head east along the rocky path, turn to **82**.

2

You stand back, and take a look at whatever it was that set itself upon you. With it laying in a crumpled heap upon the ground, you think that it is dead at first – yet despite the lengthy fall, the thing rises to its feet in only seconds, and fixes you with a spine-chilling glare. Whilst it may appear human in shape, a single look is enough to show that it is, in actuality, a reanimated corpse.

Undead Guardian
HP: 15
Attack: 5
Defence: 3

ENEMY ENCOUNTER

If you win the fight, turn to **89**. If you lose, turn to **23**.

3

You cannot see past the darkness shrouding the centre of the pit, and neither can you hear any of the bricks hitting the ground. You surmise that the pit must be incredibly deep and for all you know, jumping down there could mean either dying on impact or suffering a serious injury rendering you incapable of walking. However, looking back at the undead warriors crowding around the entrance and brandishing their weapons, you swiftly decide that you'd rather take your chances in the blackness than face certain death at the hands of some reanimated monstrosities. With a great, echoing cry, you leap off of the edge, trusting your fate to gravity. To find what awaits you at the pit's bottom, turn to **27**.

4

You set your gaze upon the gaping maw that is the eastern exit. Even from the middle of the hall, you can feel a draught seeping out of it, the cool air almost beckoning for you to make the long trek into the unknown. With bated breath, you step into the corridor, and begin to walk through. Every step echoes off of the walls, with only the distant sound of dripping condensation to accompany your footfalls. If you strain your ears, you can hear your own heavy breathing and thrumming heart, both rapid in the anticipation of another attack or unforeseen trap. There could be anything lurking down there in the dark — and your flashlight is nowhere near powerful enough to reveal much of any of it. To see what lays beyond the dark, turn to **197**.

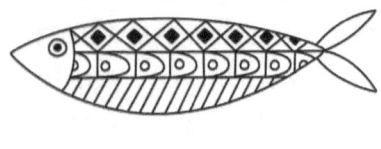

5

As you enter the northern door, it immediately becomes obvious that the room is some kind of storage area. Row upon row of jars, barrels, and sacks are stored next to and on top of each other, each one likely containing some kind of useful resource or another. It does not appear as if any of the containers have been disturbed in recent years either — aside from holes and damage seemingly caused by time and pests, both the room and its contents are blanketed by a thick layer of dust, undisturbed even by the draft that begins to fill the room when you open the door. At the far end of the room, a tall, stone cylinder rises towards the ceiling, with steps leading up towards a square hole in the front. Its purpose is, however, unclear. To examine the area further, turn to **183**. To return to the corridor, turn to **128**.

6

After all you have been through, a short rest seems like a welcome prospect – but what is revealed to you in the clearing is a far more tantalising one. The journey has been long and arduous, but at last, you have made it. Despite the doubts that many have expressed over it, the map has led you to an Inca temple, the peak of which rises high above the jungle's dense canopy. Though said canopy blocks out all but the faintest few slivers of sunlight, you can just about see a flight of steps in the distance, ostensibly carved from stone. Around you, you see nothing but the native flora of the region – trees that tower above you like giants, underbrush that hides a litany of feral beasts and swarming insects, and assortments of flowers whose poisons are likely no less deadly than the animals you suspect are lurking nearby. Having taken stock of your situation, you must now begin your exploration in earnest – though perhaps it would be best to take a closer look at your surroundings, and see if there is anything else that should be noted before you start towards the temple. To examine the area further, turn to **85**. To go to the temple steps, turn to **184**.

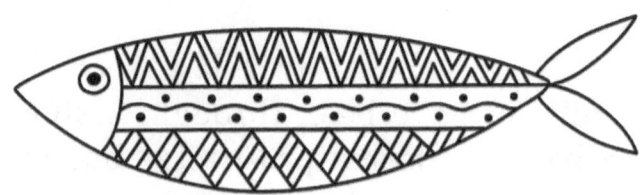

7

Eventually, the density of the plants begins to thin out – though this doesn't mean that they stop completely. Both your clothes and your pack manage to snag on a few stray branches and vines reaching out into your chosen route, almost sending you stumbling into the undergrowth more than once. Long before you reach the point where the vegetation is thinnest, you hear the sound of rushing water. And, after emerging onto a rocky ledge, the cause is plain to see. Cutting through the ground in front of you, and flowing so fast that little can be seen of the surface past the white foam frothing against the rocks, is a stream. To examine the area further, turn to **152**. To jump across the stream, turn to **13**. To climb down the steep ledge, turn to **123**.

8

Taking a closer look at the room, you see that the piles of hay stacked around the room are all roughly human-sized, as if arranged into makeshift beds. Each one is covered with a blanket, with each of those in turn being in various states of decay. Some blankets, beside their musty smell and stains, appear to be more or less intact. Others are little more than moth-eaten scraps, resembling nets more than anything designed to actually provide comfort. Strangely enough though, one appears to be in perfect condition, save for whatever dust has managed to settle upon its surface.

ITEM AVAILABLE

Blanket: A blanket that is strangely cool to the touch. Found amidst a room full of blankets in various states of decay and disrepair.

To move forward, turn to **75**. To head back, turn to **65**.

9

You step backwards, brace yourself, then run straight towards the river's edge. Miraculously, you do not slip at any stage of the run-up, and with expert form, you send yourself flying off of the riverbank. Not-so-miraculously, you find halfway through your arc that you aren't anywhere near adept enough at long-jumping to make it even halfway across the river. You have little time to reflect on this before the current slams you against a rock, granting you a painful and rather unceremonious end.

GAME OVER – BETTER LUCK NEXT TIME!

10

The lich's might was great, and its mastery over the arcane arts a sight to behold – but was still felled by you. With one last screech, it falls to the ground, leaving you to pick through its remains to find anything worth taking. The clothes, while they may once have been a sign of immense wealth due to their pigment and quality, are not worth much to you. Though a scholar of some stripe or another may have frothed at the mouth at the chance to examine such an item, you doubt that you could find a buyer that would pay more for it than someone would for the other items the lich has left behind. You examine the jewellery the abomination once wore, and turn it over in your hands, inspecting every inch. Without an expert on hand, you cannot say for certain what each piece's true value is, but it is clear from a single glance that even one would fetch a king's ransom at the bare minimum. Forged from the purest gold and decorated with gems polished and cut into a dazzling array of colours, every piece is quite obviously the work of an artist without peer. The materials alone would be enough to leave you set for life, but with the work performed on them? You struggle even to imagine the sum they would go for at auction. Then there is the matter of the staff. As fine a piece of craftsmanship as the wood is – along with its metal gilding – neither are the true appeal of the weapon. It is the gem set into the top of the staff that draws your eye. As brilliant a blue as the sky, as cleanly cut as any modern gem, and without a single imperfection, its quality alone would guarantee an astounding figure. But this is all compounded by the sheer size of it. Were you to clasp both of your hands together into a single fist, the gemstone would still be larger. There can be no doubt that the price it would command at auction would be astronomical.

ITEMS AVAILABLE

Lich Emperor's Jewellery: A set of golden jewellery, beset with all kinds of different gemstones. Forged from the purest gold and crafted with peerless expertise, a full set would command immense wealth.

Lich Emperor's Staff: An enormous gemstone set into a golden staff, cut perfectly, and with any imperfections removed from its surface. With its size, quality, and craftsmanship, even an untrained eye can tell that it is valuable beyond belief.

To approach the southern door, turn to **74**.

11

You turn to make your way through the jungle, but before you have the chance, something knocks you flat against the floor, and begins to claw at your body. By some miracle, you manage to wrench yourself out of your attack's grasp and take stock of it, though you do not emerge from the struggle unscathed. Standing, and locking eyes with your attacker, you see that you have been ambushed by a jaguar – and it doesn't look to be a particularly friendly one either. To fight the jaguar, turn to **41**. To try and scare the jaguar away, turn to **92**. To run away from the jaguar, turn to **30**.

12

You turn your attention towards the looming darkness that lays beyond the hall's western exit, and to the titans that stand on either side of it. Unlike the clay behemoth that you faced earlier, the statues show no sign of life. Looking closely, you note the vines creeping through the cracks behind them, snaking slowly across the floor towards the plinths on which they are mounted. You are certain that historians and archaeologists would be in awe of them, but you decide that it would be best to move on and seek out treasures you can actually bring with you. To venture into the darkness beyond the eagle statues, turn to **164**.

13

After you take a few steps back to give yourself room for a running start, you rush in and leap forward. For a few moments, it seems that you will be able to close the distance – the ledge is steep, and gives you plenty of time to make the leap. As you descend quickly towards the rocks however, you see that it wasn't anywhere near enough – and even if it had been, leaping from such a height was a terrible idea in the first place. You take some small comfort in knowing that you don't have to endure the pain of broken legs, as you are dashed viciously against the rocks head-first, killing you instantly.

GAME OVER – BETTER LUCK NEXT TIME!

14

You turn to the west, and begin to tread down the 'path' through the trees. The gaps between them aren't particularly wide, but they're enough for you to get past without too much trouble – even if your clothes and your pack manage to snag on the odd branch or vine. Further in, you come across yet another split in the route – or, rather, two long stretches of ground that aren't *so* dense that you can't get through them without getting yourself stuck between two trees. You can't see too far down either, with the vegetation keeping the distance obscured. It becomes clear that you will need to head down either path to figure them out. To head along the western path, turn to **77**. To go along the southern path instead, turn to **143**.

15

After what seems to be an age, traversing more twists and turns than you could possibly keep track of, you see the tiniest glimmer of light at the end of the corridor. It is faint, and it is only visible because of the darkness plaguing the rest of the maze... yet nonetheless, it *is* there. Glad to finally have found what seems like an exit, you make haste towards the end of your ordeal, flashlight held outstretched in front of you – just in case there are any traps waiting to be sprung that you haven't detected yet. To head towards the light, turn to **195**.

16

You return along the path you came from, and take a look upon the area where the paths branch out. As far as clearings go, the one you are in seems to be fairly small – just wide enough for there to be different routes connected to it, but not enough to hold anything else of any significance. From there, you get your bearings, and look around at the options that are available to you. If you have the **Machete** and wish to go south, turn to **21**. To head westwards along the flat path, turn to **14**. Or, if you want to try the rocky path to the east, turn to **82**.

17

You shine your torch against the fungi, and examine them closely. While the cluster appears to be far larger than any of the others dotted around the cavern, there is nothing you see about them on a first glance to indicate that they are worth taking with you. Not that you have the option of studying them any further, though – a shadow creeping up behind you sees to that. With all due haste, you turn quickly around, and see that the statue to the side of the corridor has sprung to life, but you do not notice quickly enough to block or dodge its strike, and it scores a savage hit against you – take **5** damage instantly. To fight the statue, turn to **88**. To run away, turn to **120**.

You take the stone key from your pack, pressing the end firmly against the hole. It is a perfect fit; with little more than a light push it slides easily into the stone block, the action punctuated by an unceremonious click. A moment of silence fills the air, followed shortly by a grinding coming from around the hole you have now filled. The block pulls back an inch or two, before sinking slowly into the bricks beneath it, gradually vanishing with the sound of stone grating against stone. An empty space is revealed: a small alcove, into which you shine your flashlight in order to better investigate its contents. Interestingly, you can see that the gap holds more than just dirt and dust, as situated right in the middle of it is a brazier that blazes to life mere moments after being revealed. In the middle of the roaring flames whipping around the stone bowl, you can clearly make out a small stone statuette – no larger than your hand – that is carved expertly into the shape of an eagle. Though the bird's craftsmanship is surely exquisite, the intricate details on its body are not necessarily the most striking feature.

What draws your eyes to the eagle the most is the shining blue gem pressed into its chest and glinting in the light your flashlight casts. To remove the statuette, turn to **190**. To remove the gem, turn to **170**. If you have a **Hammer & Chisel**, turn to **162**.

19

Moving through the area, you examine the environment closely. You make progress carefully, knowing well that wet stone can be treacherous, and one slip could be fatal.

Despite the care you take, however, you can only discern two things about the river that were not immediately obvious upon your entrance. The first thing that you notice is that hidden amongst the foam and spray, rocks jut out of the river and stand firm against its flow. Some look as vicious as spears, and would surely rip you to shreds were you to so much as graze them, others seem relatively flat and unassuming. The second is the presence of a hollowed-out tree trunk laying across the breadth of the river, providing a solid-looking – if somewhat precarious – bridge across. It is even tall enough that the very top of the trunk is largely unaffected by the river's spray, only seeming a little damp instead of outright soaked through. To take a running jump over the river, turn to **9**. To step across using the rocks as a platform, turn to **201**. To use the tree trunk as a bridge, go to **108**.

20

Once the path splits, and splits again further down, you realise that it is not a straight corridor at all – it is a maze, to which you have no map. This realisation comes too late to act on, however, and the most that you can do is trudge forward. There is no way back, after all. To trudge forward through the maze, go to **187**.

21

You approach the dense thicket, and look over it before you get to work. The entire thing is so dense with vegetation that even the faintest sliver of light has difficulty finding a path through. With just enough filtering in through the canopy above, however, you are able to actually target your strikes rather than hack wildly. Each blow cuts away a portion of the green before you, and each section that falls to the ground lets you move forward another step. It's slow going, but eventually, you manage to emerge into a clearing without much blocking your way. To proceed into the clearing, turn to **38**.

22

You eventually emerge into a room that is, simply put, squalid. The stones are bare, lacking even the weeds that may normally have emerged between the cracks in the stone are absent, lending the room a deathly. A musty smell hangs in the air, plaguing the senses more and more the further you venture in. Breathing through your mouth doesn't spare you, with it being so thick that you can practically taste it as well. Despite the smell, you can make out another corridor at the far end of the room. To examine the area further, turn to **8**. To move forward, turn to **75**. To head back, turn to **65**

23

Your efforts are in vain, and the undead sentinel bests you. Darkness takes over your vision, and the last thing you can see is it reaching down to grab you by your ankles – and the last thing you can feel is it dragging you further into the temple...

GAME OVER – BETTER LUCK NEXT TIME!

24

For what seems to be an eternity, you wander aimlessly through the vast, dark expanse. You think you are going in a straight line, but with so few landmarks and such limited visibility, it is impossible to say for certain. However, you do not have to think about it – or anything else, for that matter – for long. A section of the roof drops down onto you, crushing you rather unceremoniously. Undignified an end though yours was, it was at least a quick one.

GAME OVER – BETTER LUCK NEXT TIME!

25

Slowly, you manage to lift yourself out from the water, and turn around to take stock of your situation. You surmise that the water probably deadened the sound of stone falling, and as you look up, it's clear that fall wasn't especially steep. It just seemed that way because the bottom was obscured. The darkness prompts you to check your flashlight – fortunately, it still works. As durable as it is, it wasn't made to resist something like this.

Ahead of you, you can see two paths. Where they lead is a mystery, as the darkness is simply too dense for your flashlight to pierce through. The only way to be certain about what lays where is to venture in yourself. To examine the area further, turn to **127**. To head instead down the southern path, turn to **180**. To try the western path, turn to **168**.

26

You look closely at the door, pound on it, and even utter a litany of different passphrases. But nothing works. The door remains still, barring you from escaping the undead monstrosity closing quickly in. Your attempts prove futile, and all that it does is give the lich ample opportunity to attack you once more. Take **10** damage and turn to **154**.

27

Air whips past your face, and you hurtle towards the ground. It at first seems like the fall will be your last – though the second that you slam down against the water's surface, you are filled with a small sense of relief at this stroke of good luck. Though the impact still hurts, it's at the very least not fatal. To pick yourself up and take stock of the situation, turn to **25**.

28

After eyeing the gap and evaluating the distance, you decide to risk jumping across it. A running start may be needed, but it seems like you'd be able to get across the gap so long as you push off hard enough. However, this theory is quickly disproven when you begin to descend without getting even halfway across the gap. Your feet sink into the sand in seconds, and though you try to struggle back to solid ground, the pit slows your pace to a crawl. Before you are even in arm's reach of the ledge you jumped from, you are pulled beneath the sand and left there to suffocate in its grasp.

GAME OVER – BETTER LUCK NEXT TIME!

At first, it seems as if the area immediately around you holds little of interest. Your only company is whatever vegetation can emerge through the cracks in the temple's construction, and whatever pieces of rock and rubble have come to settle against the ground. But there, at the distant end of your half of the room, you can see something resting against a wall. Your light reveals it to be a boat, constructed from reeds and made waterproof by some manner of tar, leaning against the temple's wall. It is hard to tell if it has been used recently, or even maintained – but judging by the state of the temple behind you, it would be reasonable to assume not. Intending to see what lays beyond the veil of blackness the river flows into, you shine your flashlight towards it, and peer down into its depths. And once more, your flashlight proves incapable of reaching to the bottom of the path – but it at least serves to show what kind of dangers lay beyond. Jagged rocks as sharp as razors, currents so swift they turn the water to froth, branches hanging low enough that they would bludgeon anyone unfortunate enough to hit them to death –

it would take either a brave or a foolhardy soul to venture down there. However, your flashlight is at least bright enough to see to the opposite end of the room. You rake it across the ground opposite the bank you stand at, and see quickly that the floor is slick with river water, much as the ground you stand on is. It carries on for several metres, stretching on into the distance, threatening to cut off just as your light grows too dim to make out anything of significance. But then, at the edges of your flashlight's limits, you see it – a door. A heavy one, constructed from carved stone, but a door nonetheless. To jump across the river, turn to **110**. To swim downriver, turn to **99**. To try riding the reed boat downriver, turn to **107**. To ride the reed boat across the river to the other side, turn to **188**.

30

You back away from the jaguar, keeping your eyes locked firmly onto its own, contact only breaking for you to blink. Though it glares back, it doesn't make a move, instead standing still and watching you creep backwards. The air is thick with the tension between it and you, both waiting for the other to make a move – and it's you that moves first. As soon as you're far away enough from the beast, you sprint through the undergrowth, weaving and ducking between the foliage to try and shake it off of your tail, all while making headway towards whatever lays to the east. Miraculously, it soon loses interest in chasing you. While you might well have escaped it, it is more likely that it decided you simply weren't worth the energy needed to pursue. Either way, you manage to get away from it, leaving you free to move towards your next destination. To keep moving through the jungle, turn to **182**.

31

Your flashlight is stowed onto your belt, and with both hands free, you start the climb up towards the darkness. You move slowly, with even the slightest movement treated with the utmost caution, no matter how secure you think the next foothold or outcropping is going to be. You can hear rock crumbling around you, echoing in the distance. Chunks of it tumble down into whatever other pits exist past your own, the sounds of it faint but the air still enough that you manage to hear it nevertheless. Perhaps it is simply the passage of time taking its toll; perhaps it is a grim portent of what is to come. Only time will tell. To keep moving upwards, turn to **49**.

32

The very moment that you step through the door, you find the floor beneath you parting, and dropping you several feet into the mud below. Luckily, the dirt is enough to keep you from taking any serious injuries – but even if you could climb back up the sheer wall of stone behind you, the floor closing up would likely not part for you again. It seems that the only thing to do is to press forward. To move through the mud, turn to **149**.

33

The journey upwards is long, and leaves you with more than a few bumps and scrapes to show for it. Though the uneven surface of the wall is a godsend as a makeshift handrail to keep a hold of, it also digs into your sides, threatening to slice at both your clothes and skin like knives. The ground is dry and coarse enough to provide a decent surface for your boots to grip onto, though parts of it give way under your weight – not enough to send you stumbling back, but enough that the risk always seems to loom over your head. The journey does not end there either. Even as the jagged walls begin to smooth out into what feels like the stone slabs of the temple proper, your probing grasp eventually comes across something that feels like a vine or rope hanging down, moving only from the draught blowing in from above. Thankfully, it feels solid enough to hold your weight. Just as well, given that it is the only way up. You climb up, and what seems to have been an age of fumbling around in the dark finally comes to an end. The ground ahead levels out and the tunnel now widens into another cavern. Turn to **103**.

34

Though it is a little touch and go at times, the rest of the jumps go surprisingly well. Each careful step forward puts you closer to the opposite edge of the cavern, until eventually you manage to make one final push towards solid ground more than half a metre wide. To move forward towards the other end of the cave, turn to **69**.

35

It isn't long before the tunnel leads out into a dark room, filled with that distinct sound of sand shifting in place. A quick look with your flashlight is all you need to find the source. Beyond the sand-covered rock, a vast pit of sand reaches towards the solid ground at the other end of the cavern. Somehow, it never seems to stop shifting, sinking, and changing – like the currents of the ocean, just waiting for some hapless traveller to fall in and be dragged to their untimely demise. You know not how deep the sand is, but suspect it will likely be enough to kill you. And not pleasantly either. To examine the area further, turn to **90**. To jump across the pit, turn to **28**.

36

After a few minutes of trudging down the empty corridor, you come upon a split in the path. Each one leads in a different direction – though if the symbol on the ground is any indication, there is only one correct path forwards. Despite your previous decision not to heed the warning given by the carving on the ground, you make the choice to set off down the path that this one indicates. To continue down this path, turn to **163**.

37

Further examination of the area reveals little information of use. The most you can confirm about the room is that it is just as big as you suspected it to be. Traversing its length and breadth takes an age, and the darkness that each exit is plagued by reaches too far for your flashlight to reveal anything meaningful. To go through the eastern exit, turn to **4**. To try the western exit instead, turn to **12**.

38

You step forwards and look around at the jungle clearing surrounding you. The ground is flat enough that you can walk over it without much trouble. Moreover, as far as you can tell, the flora – while thick – is dense enough that you can push it out of the way instead of cutting it, should you wish to continue further along the route you've chosen. To examine the clearing further, turn to **114**. To continue along the route, turn to **11**.

39

Just like the statues in the rooms before you, the carved eagles to either side remain as still as stone. Not only do they seem disinclined to attack, but they are also too heavy for you to move either; it seems that, barring some unfortunate turn of events, they will remain in place for the foreseeable future. The floor, meanwhile, holds something that may be of more interest: a glyph, etched into the stone. It is clearly not a pattern worn into the ground by the passage of time, and is something left there by man. As you have no reference for what it means at present, you decide to make a mental note of it, and proceed forwards. To go through the left door, turn to **191**. To head through the middle door, turn to **112**. Or, if you'd like to try the right-hand door, turn to **96**.

40

Slowly, you drag the flashlight's glare across the edges of the corridor's entrance. In a stark contrast to the parts of the temple closer to the surface, the ones here appear to have been carved recently. There's little sign of the wear and tear that plagues the art higher up – as if someone had only just finished smoothing out any cracks or crevices, and touched up the patterns with a careful eye. But before you can deduce anything from the carvings, something arcs through the air behind you, and lands a vicious blow. Hurt, you turn swiftly around to find the cause – only to see that the statue has come to life without you noticing. You can do nothing to avoid taking a blow that knocks the wind out of you; take **5** damage. To fight the statue, turn to **88**. Or, to run away, turn to **120**.

41

You stand before the jaguar, looking at it closely, while moving slowly to try and find a more advantageous position. The beast does the same, prowling across the ground while fixing you with a savage glare. Though shorter, every inch of it seems to be muscle, lending both its claws and its teeth awesome power.

Jaguar
HP: 10
Attack: 5
Defence: 1

ENEMY ENCOUNTER

If you win, turn to **121**, or to **140** if you lose.

42

You observe the ebb and flow of the stream, watch its currents, and calculate precisely how much force you need to jump onto the rocks poking out above the surface. This proves fruitless when you slip on the damp surface and instead slam into the rocks you thought you could jump across.

GAME OVER – BETTER LUCK NEXT TIME!

43

You look behind you, and at the other doors branching off from the corridor. All except the one leading towards the exit have been closed off, sealed by stone – and not the damaged sort that you might be able break through. With no other paths to try, there is really only one route left available and that is towards the temple's exit. To leave the temple behind, turn to **79**.

44

After pulling yourself and your pack through the gap, you emerge into a dank, unlit room plagued by the smell of withered fabrics and vegetation left to rot. Under normal circumstances, being in an abandoned environment like this would have been somewhat eerie, with the fear that you could be assaulted at any second by something lurking in the dark. But now, knowing how the lower and cleaner levels are what house the temple's true horrors, you cannot help but feel a slight sense of relief upon seeing the state that this part of the temple has been left in. At the very least, it means that you're on the right track. As you cast your light around the room, you realise where exactly you have ended up. The jars, the sacks, the dearth of any kind of decoration save for them – it is clear that this is where you got the stone key from, early on in your journey through the temple. To keep moving through the temple, turn to **186**.

45

The second that you move past the door, it once again slams back into place. No matter what you do to or with it, the door remains in its position, stoic and unmoving. With no way back to the throne room – and little chance anything will come through after you – you walk along the corridor to the next room. To see what is past the throne room, turn to **101**.

46

After picking yourself up from your slide down towards the stream's edge, you look around to take stock of the situation. At first glance, the area appears to be much the same as how you imagined it would be. The only real difference between the impression you got from the ledge and the one you have from here down below is the spray from the raging current – and it's only that the spray is a lot more intense than you had first thought it would be. To examine the area further, turn to **59**. To jump across using the rocks, turn to **42**. To swim across the stream, turn to **165**.

47

As you turn back to return to the hall from which you came, part of the floor gives way, and sinks beneath your foot. Far too late, you figure out that it is a pressure plate; no sooner do you realise you have activated it than you hear a metallic clanging ringing throughout the room. All you can do is watch as a giant, golden beast comes lumbering through the corridor, its metal body causing every step taken to sound throughout the temple like a great bell. Behind it, the sound of sliding stone signals an impossibly large slab being pushed out from the edge of the corridor's frame and blocking your one and only way out. With no other exits available, you must stand and fight the new enemy.

Golden Guardian
HP: 15
Attack: 7
Defence: 3

ENEMY ENCOUNTER

If you win the fight, turn to **178**, or if you lose, turn to **176**.

48

You are only too glad to get away from the room, and whatever it contained. And while the corridor you are now pacing down is far from the most pleasant place in the world, it is a far sight better than the torture chamber you leave behind. Hopefully, the next room leads to a way out – or, at the very least, something markedly less grim. To see what lies ahead, turn to **130**.

49

You do not know how long it has taken, but eventually the wall levels out into a ledge. Though it is smooth, you manage to grip onto it enough to pull yourself onto flat ground. Now able to use your flashlight again, you grab it off your belt and sweep it around the new cavern you find yourself in. Barring the lack of a passage upwards, the walls, floor and ceiling look near-identical to the place you have just left behind. The stone around you is a dull shade of grey, bereft of man's touch — whatever patterns or designs are present on it are entirely natural, formed only by the passage of time. The ceiling is the same, lacking any features worth mentioning besides its stability... including a passage onwards to the surface. As for the hole from which you have emerged, you know what lays below it, and have no desire to venture back down. Eventually, you take a more detailed investigation around the cavern, and find an opening in the wall behind you. Of course, it's another tunnel, this time with an obvious upward slant. It seems as though it should be possible to follow, as the floor is coarse enough on which to get a grip, whilst the walls have enough irregularities jutting out for you to use as holds on your way upwards. To follow the tunnel this way, turn to **33**.

50

The room you emerge into is – for the most part – empty. Two more eagle statues stand on either side of you as you enter, while at the far end, three wooden doors stand tall above you. If you are to progress, you will need to figure out which of the three doors to venture through.

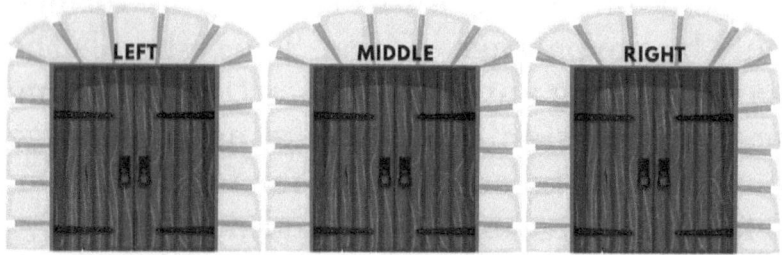

If you <u>have</u> **Notes on Eagle Statues and Carvings**, turn to **147** to investigate more, or choose:

| **172** | **102** | **175** |

If you <u>don't</u> have such notes, turn to **39** to investigate the room more. or choose:

| **191** | **112** | **96** |

49

You do not know how long it has taken, but eventually the wall levels out into a ledge. Though it is smooth, you manage to grip onto it enough to pull yourself onto flat ground. Now able to use your flashlight again, you grab it off your belt and sweep it around the new cavern you find yourself in. Barring the lack of a passage upwards, the walls, floor and ceiling look near-identical to the place you have just left behind. The stone around you is a dull shade of grey, bereft of man's touch — whatever patterns or designs are present on it are entirely natural, formed only by the passage of time. The ceiling is the same, lacking any features worth mentioning besides its stability... including a passage onwards to the surface. As for the hole from which you have emerged, you know what lays below it, and have no desire to venture back down. Eventually, you take a more detailed investigation around the cavern, and find an opening in the wall behind you. Of course, it's another tunnel, this time with an obvious upward slant. It seems as though it should be possible to follow, as the floor is coarse enough on which to get a grip, whilst the walls have enough irregularities jutting out for you to use as holds on your way upwards. To follow the tunnel this way, turn to **33**.

50

The room you emerge into is – for the most part – empty. Two more eagle statues stand on either side of you as you enter, while at the far end, three wooden doors stand tall above you. If you are to progress, you will need to figure out which of the three doors to venture through.

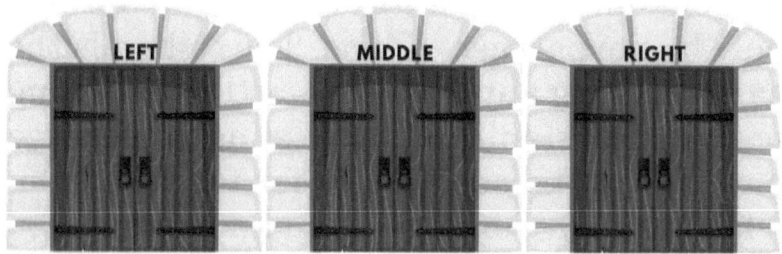

If you <u>have</u> **Notes on Eagle Statues and Carvings**, turn to **147** to investigate more, or choose:

172	**102**	**175**

If you <u>don't</u> have such notes, turn to **39** to investigate the room more. or choose:

191	**112**	**96**

52

Though the door can't be opened with brute force, the latch itself looks fairly fragile. So, rather than try and force your way past the heavy slab of stone blocking your path, you instead begin to strike the **Stick** against the latch over and over again. It takes some doing, but eventually the latch shatters into pieces which clatter unceremoniously onto the ground. With this out of the way, you are free to push against the door itself and you eventually manage to open it just enough that you can squeeze into the gap, allowing you to progress forwards and enter the temple proper. Turn to **132**.

53

With the previous room's trials behind you, you push forward once more. The layer of sand upon the ground gradually begins to wear thin, with the sound of it being stepped on growing quieter and quieter as you make headway, until the only remnant of it is that which clings to your boots. To see what is past the sand pit, turn to **157**.

51

As you emerge into yet another room along the path, you feel a sudden rush of air whip against your face. Though a little dank, it is a far less oppressive odour than that of the previous rooms. Your relief is short-lived however, as you quickly realise you are falling downwards at an alarming pace. As you hurtle towards the ground below, you glimpse the scene laid out beneath you, just about making out what seems to be an altar of some sort, littered with the dry, brittle bones of people long dead. You come to the realisation that you have fallen into a sacrificial chamber of sorts, and this is the last thing on your mind before your body breaks against the solid stone altar.

GAME OVER – BETTER LUCK NEXT TIME!

54

You start down the corridor leading to the west. While largely empty, it is decorated far more lavishly and is illuminated by torches that light up as you pass them by. Rather than just the usual assortment of patterns carved into the stone and what remains of faded paint, not an inch of the corridor is without some manner of gold. Be it a statue, an inlay, or simply the flakes left behind from making either, the entire place holds a small fortune in the stuff. Unfortunately, the statues are simply too heavy and bulky to take with you, the inlays are set too deep to pry out and the flakes really aren't worth the effort required to gather them up. It's best just to move on. Turn to **192**.

55

As you inspect the corridor further, you find what appears to be a jar full of artist's supplies. Sadly, almost every single item has been rendered useless by the ravages of time. The brushes are too stiff to paint anything with and most of the tools too dull to do much more than scratch a shallow mark into the stone, assuming they don't break before it happens. The only thing that seems to be capable of performing its function is a **Hammer and Chisel** set, though the chisel doesn't look as if it would survive more than a few bashes and the handle of the hammer has suffered from water damage. Nevertheless, the set is small and light enough to fit into your pack without much issue, so you may pick it up. With the corridor thoroughly examined, you turn your attention back towards the three passages available to you.

ITEM AVAILABLE

Hammer & Chisel Set: A hammer and chisel. Too small and fragile to use as weapons, but perfect for etching into stone. Just don't bash the chisel too hard or it'll instantly fall apart.

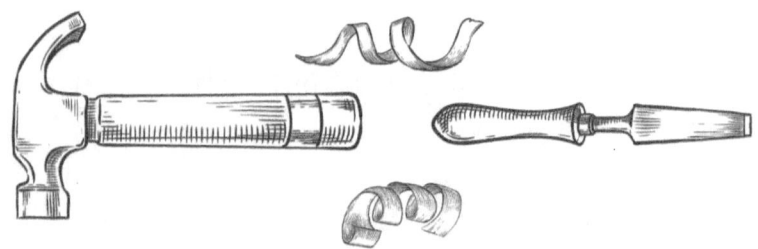

Now, which way will you go? To try the northern door, turn to **5**. To go through the southern door, you should turn to **136**. To continue westwards, turn to **111**.

56

The river levels out and the danger of being dashed against the rocks passes... but now is not the time to relax. The jagged edges that threatened to shred you apart have simply given way to an entirely different manner of danger. There, in the distance, you can see gouts of flame surging down from the temple ceiling. Piped in through narrow stone passageways, the fire burns bright, filling the path ahead with light – and with searing heat. Even from the distance you are at, you can tell that failing to act in time will leave you as little more than smouldering ashes. To duck under the flames, turn to **60**. To jump into the water, turn to **189**. If you want to cover yourself with the **Blanket**, turn to **76**.

57

After what seems to have been an age, you emerge from the corridor. To call what lays beyond the threshold a mere room would be to do it a disservice, however. Even describing it as a hall would barely scratch the surface of this part of the underground temple's awe-inspiring majesty. The area set out before you is simply gargantuan. Smooth, expertly-hewn bricks stretch across the floor as far as the eye can see, and reach far higher than your flashlight's glow can manage. The ceiling — wherever it may be in the impenetrable darkness above — is supported by titanic stone pillars, each one of them standing as tall as the massive trees outside the temple proper. The walls that surround you are cut from the same stone as the pillars, and — like the pillars they stand behind — rise far higher than your meagre tools are capable of reaching. Every aspect of the room dwarfs you, as though you were no more than an ant scurrying about, nothing but an insignificant insect trapped within its depths. Besides the entrance that lays behind you, the room holds towering passageways, each one a yawning chasm unto itself.

However, despite how well-preserved much of the temple seems to be, all but two of the available passages have collapsed leaving just one in the east, and one to the west. The western exit is towered over by two eagles, both fashioned from blocks of solid stone. Unlike the statue before, neither are adorned with any manner of gem – upon first glance, both seem to be simple stone statues. The eastern exit holds no statues. Instead, a pattern runs across the frame surrounding it – and through that runs a golden inlay. As your flashlight catches against the frame, it gleams brilliantly, shining bright amidst the looming darkness that surrounds you at every turn. To examine the area further, turn to **37**. To go through the eastern door, turn to **4**. If, instead, you fancy your chances to the west, turn to **12**.

58

You progress through the maze, making sure to refer back to your notes at every turn to determine which path is the correct one. However, despite making certain to follow the directions set out by the symbols etched into the ground, you still manage to trigger a pressure plate at a dead end. You barely have time to reflect on what the correct choice may have been before you are dumped unceremoniously into a pit filled with razor-sharp spikes – though it is *just* enough that you feel like an idiot for make the wrong choice, regardless.

GAME OVER – BETTER LUCK NEXT TIME!

59

A more thorough examination of the stream reveals little, aside from the fact that getting pelted in the face by a larger river's castoffs is exceptionally unpleasant. However, looking past the bank and ground around you, there are a couple of other more promising, prospects. One of them is a dead tree. Though it has been decaying long enough that the wood itself is weakened and grown over by all manner of different flora, what little of it is exposed does not seem to have completely succumbed to rot. With enough force, you could probably break away parts, along with some of the vines wrapping around it. Doing so would allow you to create a makeshift raft – nothing fancy or durable, but likely enough to get across the stream with. The other thing that catches your eye is a large branch. Though thinner, it seems to have only recently fallen and appears to be wide enough to walk along. Moving it will likely be a challenge as it is still fairly heavy-looking, but you might still be able to use it as a makeshift bridge. To jump across using the rocks, turn to **42**. To swim across the stream, turn to **165**. To use the fallen tree as a bridge, turn to **84**, or if you have the **Machete** and wish to make a raft, turn to **126**.

60

You crouch and put your hands above your head, hoping that the fire will not reach far down enough to injure you – or, at the very least, that it will not hurt too much when you pass through it. You quickly find out that your hopes are in vain. The moment that you draw close, the flames cover you and reduce both the boat and its passenger to little more than cinders drifting on the water's surface.

GAME OVER – BETTER LUCK NEXT TIME!

61

As if recognising your victory over the **Undead Guardian**, the door begins to shake as you approach it. It quakes in place, filling the hall with a deafening rumbling noise, before finally beginning to move. Slowly, it sinks into the temple's floor and gradually reveals that which lays beyond it. Like so many of the passageways before however, the one beyond the hall's western door remains shrouded in darkness. It seems that, beyond using a brighter flashlight, the only way to see what lies on the other side is to venture in and see it for yourself. To make your way through the western door, turn to **54**.

62

Fortunately, your flashlight still works and you sweep it across the landscape set out before you. You appear to be in some kind of underground cavern, untouched by man save for the stone pipes mounted into the ceiling further back. Craggy stone walls rise high above the ground, slick from the spray of water frothing up from the river behind you.

The combination of darkness and dampness means that the only other inhabitants here are fungi and particularly stubborn weeds. All in all, there is little in the way of life, save for you. However, you can see something in the distance... another corridor. There is no mistaking the stone slabs lining that rectangular entryway, nor the statue standing to its side as if to guard against erstwhile intruders. With nowhere else left to go, you trudge forward and make your way towards the only path available; turn to **146**.

63

The very second that you step through the door, a great slab of stone slams down behind you. Just a glance at it is enough to tell you that there is no way that you are going to be able to get past it – certainly not without a lot of explosives. The only way remaining is forwards... though quite where 'forwards' may be is hard to tell, as the entire room before you is empty. Not just in the way it lacks any kind of decoration or that its furnishings are spartan; the room simply has nothing in it. There is no furniture, no light and not even any walls that you can make our from where you stand. No matter in which direction you look, all that your flashlight shows is murky blackness. To begin your trek through the unknown, turn to **72**.

The statue eventually crumbles against your might. The last of your hits causes it to freeze in place before juddering violently and cracking from the point of impact outwards. As the last of the cracks finally reaches the edge of its body, the entire thing crumbles into a pile of clay powder, interspersed with shards of stone. Hidden in the rubble left behind, three objects catch the light of your flashlight, glinting amidst the dark. Closer inspection reveals them to be gemstones – raw and uncut, but polished and of quite a size too. While the smaller two were acting as its eyes, the larger of the three hadn't been visible through the entire fight. You surmise that it was probably hidden within the statue's body the entire time – though to what end, you can only guess at.

ITEM AVAILABLE

Statue Gems: A set of three gems, obtained from a defeated Clay Guardian. Two are about the size of an adult's eyeballs, while one is as large as a man's heart.

To proceed down the corridor, turn to **57**.

65

The grinding of stone fills the air as you step out into the temple's interior, and a massive door rises to fill the gap that was once the corridor's entrance. Just a glance at it is enough to tell you that there is no way you will make it through – it would take far stronger tools than you can carry to get past it. Only the western passage is available to you now, and whatever is behind the eastern door has now been locked away. To go west, turn to **128.**

66

Using what little of the raft is left, you leap towards solid ground. Your efforts are just enough to save you – your heels land barely an inch from the water. Nevertheless, you have made it to the other side of the stream, and can move on with your journey. To keep moving through the jungle, turn to **182.**

At first, the shelves appear to hold little of interest. However, as you look closer, you see the glare of your flashlight catch on something shiny in a torn sack – something metallic. Opening it up, you see exactly what the metallic glint was: a brick, made from solid gold. But that is just the tip of the iceberg. Every sack reveals a different treasure, from jewellery to statuettes with precious stones embedded across their surfaces. The room is more than just some dusty old storeroom behind the throne; it is a treasury, packed with valuable antiquities that could set a man up for life several times over.

ITEMS AVAILABLE

Gold Brick: A brick made from solid gold. Though heavy, it is quite literally worth its weight in gold and will fetch a hefty price from the right buyer.

Gold Jewellery: Rings, necklaces, bracelets, and other such trinkets – all beset with a litany of jewels. Valuable to collectors and scholars alike, both for their materials and historical value.

Gold Statue: statue resembling a person, made from solid gold and embedded with jewels. Made more valuable than the sum of its parts by the craftsmanship and history behind it.

Gold Coins: A collection of loose coins. Likely used more as a tool to barter with European settlers than with the Incas themselves.

Gold Eagle: A statue resembling an eagle, forged from solid gold and embedded with jewels. The craftsmanship and history behind it lend it immense value.

Make your choice as to which items to take, ensuring you either have or make room for them in your backpack. After doing this, it's time to investigate the walls; turn to **158**.

68

After you stow your flashlight on your belt to free up your hands – though still keeping it within reach should the need arise – you creep down the wall. Each movement is made slowly, and with the utmost caution; there is no telling how far the fall is, or what awaits at the bottom. Turn to **83**.

69

Now safely on the other side, you take stock of the situation around you – though from what you can see, it doesn't seem like there's much here that is worth noting either. There are no stone slabs, no carvings, no guardians nor liches; the network of caverns and tunnels you have found yourself in seem to be entirely separate to the temple. With nothing else to see on this side of the pit, you decide it's best to move on. Turn to **53**.

70

With a burst of adrenaline-driven speed, you make a mad dash towards the exit. Surprisingly, none of the reanimated warriors present are quick enough to stop you, but it quickly becomes apparent that they don't need to – the exit back into the throne room is still sealed shut, and there's no way for you to break through it. You only just have enough time to turn around and see the oncoming horde before they hack you apart.

GAME OVER – BETTER LUCK NEXT TIME!

71

As you step forward, your flashlight sweeps across the area in front of you. The light only reveals a dead end, however, and you turn around to make your way back to a different path – or, at least, you try. Before you know it, you find yourself sinking down to your waist, falling ever-deeper into the muddy depths. No matter how you claw or struggle, you are unable to pull yourself even an inch higher, and you soon find yourself condemned to a muddy grave.

GAME OVER – BETTER LUCK NEXT TIME!

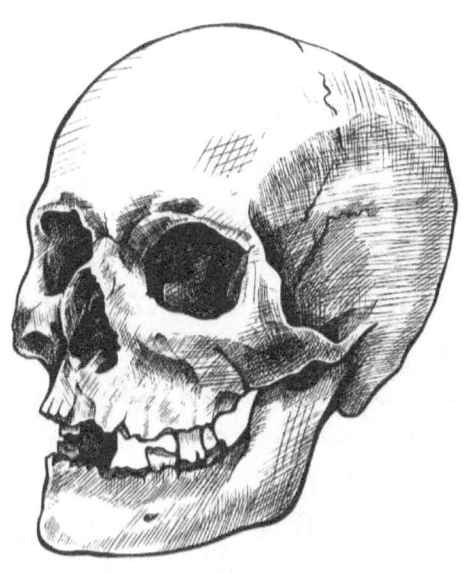

72

Your footsteps echo throughout the area. Save for your breathing and the rapid pounding of your heart, they are the only sounds that can be heard amidst the room's deathly silence. The thrumming of your heart only grows more intense as it becomes clear that you are hopelessly lost; only the room's pillars are there to serve as waypoints. Although the odd glyphs help to distinguish them thus providing somewhat of a landmark, they do little to tell you which direction you actually need to head in to escape. To explore the empty area further, turn to **24**.

73

You raise your weapon, and strike hard against the hole. Little by little, the stone begins to chip away, until it finally crumbles and falls to the floor as little more than a pile of rubble. However, you are not given the chance to examine what lies beyond it, as forcing an opening has had the unfortunate effect of setting off one of the temple's traps. The ground opens up beneath you like a gaping maw, and before you even have the chance to process what is happening, you are dumped unceremoniously into the bowels of the earth, where you meet your grisly fate with a dull, echoing, thud.

GAME OVER – BETTER LUCK NEXT TIME!

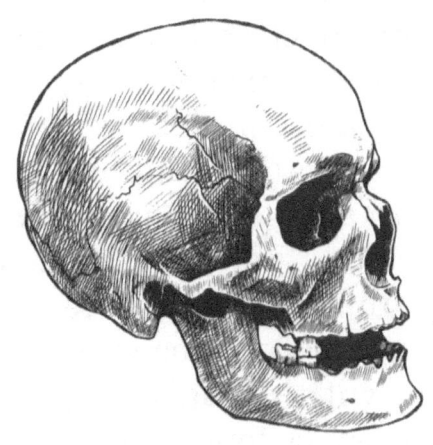

74

You approach the door, but before you have a chance to examine it, the entire thing falls into the floor. It seems that, in recognition of your victory over the emperor, it has opened for you. As it is the only way forward, you step across the threshold, and begin to make your way to whatever lies beyond. To move away from the throne room, turn to **45**.

75

Much like the room before it, the area into which you emerge is infested by a disgusting stench that threatens to choke anyone foolish enough to venture in deeper. Despite this, you continue on into the room and gaze around at whatever it has to offer. In a stark contrast to the previous area, this one is decorated quite lavishly. Intricate and detailed patterns are carved into the walls, winding around their length and breadth and only interrupted by the next corridor. Similar patterns are etched into a stone plinth in the centre of the room, while yet another corridor stands at the far end – again, with no light to provide hints on what may lay beyond. If you can bear the smell, you could take a closer look around – in which case, turn to **138**. To move forward, turn to **51**, or to head back the way you came, turn to **65**.

76

You rip the blanket from your pack, wet it in the water and only just have enough time to cover yourself with it before the current brings you right underneath the flames. Curled up in the foetal position, you wait and wait, bracing yourself for the burning heat of the fire erupting from the ceiling, only to feel... nothing. Eventually, you decide to take a chance, and look out from underneath the blanket. As you glance around, it quickly becomes apparent that you have long since passed by the flames – in fact, you are far enough past them that you cannot even feel their heat. It seems that the wet blanket was enough of a shield from the flames that you made it through the temple's fiery trap. Unfortunately, the reeds of your boat that remained uncovered were not so lucky and are now aflame. Knowing that what is left of the boat will soon be unable to support your weight, you are forced to abandon it. Fortunately, you are close enough to the bank that with a couple of strokes you make it to safety. It is a good thing you did, as when you look back, all you can see is a rapidly-sinking tangle of tarred reeds, burning and smouldering as they drift along with the current. You take a few moments to compose yourself before taking stock of the situation. Having calmed yourself down, you can now turn to **62**.

77

The further along the path you go, the thinner the surrounding of trees seems to get. The rest of the flora seem to follow suit, until finally, growth of anything seems to stop completely. This is hardly a surprise, as the path leads to a rocky ledge, overlooking yet more jungle. To see if there is anything of interest on the ledge, turn to **133**.

78

You examine the room more closely, but make sure to keep an eye out behind you to prevent a repeat of the earlier incident. While it initially seems as though the statues are disinclined to spring to life, the **Clay Guardian** was trouble enough on its own. There is no such thing as being too careful where a whole room full of stone sentinels is concerned. Fortunately, you are allowed to study the room in peace, though it seems as though the eagle statues are the only points of interest in the immediate vicinity. Studying them closer, you surmise there might be something in the directions they face and the symbols etched into the platforms on which they stand. After a few minutes of comparing different statues across the room, you are certain of it: there is a pattern, and it's that each symbol corresponds to a different direction. Quite what implication this has on the rest of the temple, you are unsure, but you make certain to take down **Notes on Eagle Statues and Carvings** for future reference, and continue down the hall. Turn to **166**.

79

Your steps echo through the temple's still, dust-ridden air, their sound bouncing off each and every stone around you. Despite your exhaustion, the weight of your supplies, and all of your gear being torn, sodden or both, you manage to drag yourself gradually towards the temple's exit. Eventually, you can see something in the distance: *light*. Not a torch, not a flashlight, but natural light filtering in through a gap in the temple's construction. With one last burst of energy, you rush forwards, your focus shifting entirely towards it. It isn't long before sunlight hits your eyes, and you feel the warmth from the outside world wash over your skin. The brightness is enough to stun you and the air is immensely humid – yet you have never been so relieved to have either. You have found your way through the temple, and escaped the **INCA CURSE**. Congratulations! Turn to **206** to find out what happens next.

80

A more thorough examination of the room reveals exactly what goods are on offer for you to take. Valuable as the furniture may be, each piece would be too cumbersome to carry, and breaking them apart would reduce their value significantly. Instead, your focus turns to the other pieces around the room, each promising an easier time when hauling them to the surface. Jars, vases and boxes lined up against the wall contain an assortment of valuables. Some hold masterfully-crafted jewellery, including bangles, necklaces and parts of head-dresses, glistening brightly under the orange light from the torches above.

The shining gold contains a litany of gems, expertly carved and polished so well you can see your reflection staring back at you from their gleaming surfaces. More containers still present to you golden blocks, coins and assorted stones so dense and pure that even a single handful of any is sure to leave you walking away with a staggering sum. On the other side of the room is a rack with an array of weapons. Like the rest of the artefacts contained within the room, every single one of them is in perfect condition. With edges keen enough to cut you with just a look, and hafts as solid and sturdy as the trees they were cut from, it is a near certainty that they will prove a match for any enemy that may henceforth cross your path. Shields also hang at either side of the rack, made from wood strong enough to rival metal.

ITEMS AVAILABLE

Raw Gems: Unprocessed gems of every kind. Some are as small as the tip of a finger, while others are the size of a fist.

Gold Ore: Unprocessed gold ore. While not as valuable or efficient to carry as processed gold, it is still better than nothing.

Gold Bricks: A set of bricks made from gold. Though heavy, they are quite literally worth their weight in gold, and will fetch a hefty price with the right buyer.

Gold Coins: A collection of loose coins. Likely used more as a tool to barter with European settlers than with the Incas themselves.

Gold Jewellery: Rings, necklaces, bracelets, and other such trinkets – all beset with a litany of jewels. Valuable to collectors and scholars alike, both for their materials and historical value.

Emperor's Mace: A spiked head forged from an extremely durable metal, attached to a wooden haft. Its heft and balance are uncanny – as if it was made for you to hold. **+5** to attack rolls.

Emperor's Spear: A durable metal head honed to a vicious point and attached to a long pole hewn from sturdy wood. Just one strike seems like it would be enough to pierce through even the strongest armour. **+7** to attack rolls, but takes up two inventory slots.

Emperor's Small Shield: A square of expertly-crafted wood, so strong that it feels as sturdy as steel – but nowhere near as heavy. **-3** to enemy attack rolls.

Emperor's Large Shield: A rectangle of expertly-crafted wood, so strong that it feels as sturdy as steel – but nowhere near as heavy. -5 to enemy attack rolls, but takes up two inventory slots.

To move back into the hall, turn to **15**.

81

As you step into the next room, the stench of death surrounds you, and dominates your senses almost immediately. Opening your mouth does little to avail you – the smell is strong enough that doing so merely lets a disgusting taste linger upon your tongue. Your eyes begin to water at the foul odour, but despite the tears you can just about discern what the room contains... though none of it is pleasant. Cages hang from the ceiling, swinging gently in the cool draught filling the room. Manacles line the walls, hammered in so far that even with the damage caused by the passage of time, no human could ever hope to wrench themselves free from the restraints, however hard they should struggle against them. Tattered ropes snake across the floor, with the remains of what had once been knots now rotting away into nothingness. Nauseatingly, in every restraint and at the end of every rope, lie bones: piles and piles of human remains, long since turned brittle. The room does not just reek of death, it *embodies* it. No matter which way you face, there is no life to be found – not even water coursing across the wall in singular droplets, nor weeds prying their way through the cracks in the stone. It seems that there is nothing here for you, save for the exit at the far end of the room. To examine the area further, turn to **93**, or to move on through the corridor at the far end of the room as quickly as you can, turn to **48**.

82

After weighing up the available options, you head down the path dotted with rocks. These alone don't make it too difficult to navigate through the area – they are solid, small, or flat enough that you can step on or over them without fear of slipping off of them. The problem lies in the fact that the way forward is dense with vegetation; not enough to warrant hacking it apart, but enough of an obstacle nevertheless that you are slowed significantly as you try to make your way eastwards. To continue along this path, turn to **7**, or to change your mind and head in a different direction, turn to **16**.

83

After reaching the bottom of the pit, you take out your flashlight to see what lays around you. To say that there is a dearth of features is an understatement – aside from the jagged, pointed rocks pointing upwards like a field of razors, there is nothing worth seeing down here in the pit. The only thing you can do is climb back up. Turn to **91**.

84

It takes a significant amount of strength and effort, but you manage to drag and position the fallen tree in such a way that it stretches across the breadth of the stream. Though it hardly seems to be the most stable (let alone safe) way across, you believe that the your makeshift bridge will at least hold up long enough for you to reach the other side. Whether you can return the same way is another question entirely, however. The further along you crawl, the more unstable it seems to be; while it remains still enough for you to creep across, there are too many close calls for comfort, especially with the top growing slippery from all the water lashing out and spraying onto it. To move slowly across the remainder of the tree, turn to **137**. If, on the other hand, you think it would be better to finish the crossing as quickly as you possibly can, turn to **153**.

You take a closer look at your surroundings and look for anything that you should take note of. For the most part, there is nothing that appears to be worth your attention. You recognise some fruits as edible and can hear the sound of rushing water nearby, but you have enough supplies that you do not need to resort to foraging, for now at least. What few animals you can detect are watching you, but seemingly more out of wariness at your presence than any desire to attack. There is little worth taking with you or studying closer apart from a **Stick** on the ground that could prove useful. It's long and as sturdy as they come without being too unwieldy, so you suppose that it could at least test for any unstable ground and save you from falling through it.

ITEM AVAILABLE

Stick: A long and study branch, stripped of leaves and twigs. **+1** to your attack roll.

To approach the Temple Steps, turn to **184**.

86

The door, as you had surmised from the cursory examination from the other side of the room, is a far more sturdy affair than the wooden ones seen earlier on in your journey. With no obvious mechanism to open it, and no item in your pack that appears immediately useful in resolving the situation at hand, you see that you are left with few options. However, you have come this far and can hardly justify turning back without trying anything. To jump back across the river, turn to **110**. If you want to turn back and swim downriver, turn to **99**. If you are holding a weapon and wish to strike the door, turn to **196**. Or, if you have the **Mysterious Blue Gem** and wish to hold it up to the door, turn to **198**.

87

You step past the point where the door once was, and begin your descent into the inky blackness that even your flashlight cannot pierce. Every step that you take echoes off the stone walls surrounding you, only to reverberate into the distance. The staircase seems to stretch on forever, but eventually the end is in sight – accompanied by a distinct sound of rushing water, now so close that there is no doubt it is in the next room. Turn to **135** and step into the next room.

88

Rather than turn tail and run, you decide instead to stand and fight against the living statue. Despite appearing to be constructed entirely out of rock, a closer examination shows it is actually clay... and that your enemy is far more vulnerable than it first appeared; there may be a chance you can defeat it through brute force after all.

Clay Guardian
HP: 10
Attack: 5
Defence: 1

ENEMY ENCOUNTER

If you win the fight, turn to **64**, or if you are defeated, turn to **124**.

89

Whatever magic was used to preserve the ancient Inca warrior was not enough to keep it from succumbing to your onslaught. Your attacks prove too much for it to bear and at the final strike, it lets out a shriek that slowly fades into a groan and then again into silence. A close examination of the body shows little of note, aside from the fact that whoever cast the spell successfully managed to breach the barrier between life and death and command a corpse to fight in their stead. Its weapons and armour, however, are decorated most lavishly for a mere soldier and its clothes dyed a deep shade that would have been exceedingly difficult to find or create. Most importantly for you, the spear it was wielding is made almost entirely of gold. From the tip to the end of its haft, the entire thing holds a lustrous gleam, polished so expertly that the light bouncing off it is almost enough to blind you. The weapon is inset with a number of gems, each polished to the same extent as the spear proper, and expertly cut to boot. You cannot help but be impressed by the craftsmanship – and surely value – of the weapon, even though it was just used to try and kill you.

ITEM AVAILABLE

Undead Guardian's Spear: A gleaming golden spear, beset with gems that shine just as brightly. Despite having been used as a weapon, it is – surprisingly – undamaged. **+5** to attack rolls, but takes up two inventory slots.

To recommence your journey via the western door, turn to **61**, or to head south turn to **169**.

90

Wandering about the sandy cavern, you begin to examine the environment more thoroughly, but you don't see much that you couldn't already make out from the entrance. None of the rocks nor the sand itself seem to hold anything of value, nor any particular aspect worthy of remembering. However, you do manage to discern a few rocks jutting up out of the pit. Given how many there are, and the pattern they are arranged in, there's a chance that you could use them as platforms to jump across. On the other hand, you can see a ledge jutting out from the wall which stretches around the pit's circumference; it connects both sides of the cavern and seems as though it might just be wide enough for you to squeeze across. To jump across the pit in one huge leap, turn to **28**. To try a series of smaller hops across the more prominent rocks, turn to **181**. Or to attempt to sidle around the ledge, turn to **23**.

91

With nothing in the pit worth examining further, you begin the long climb back up. Once more, your flashlight is stowed, and once more you sink your foot against whatever caps and outcrops you can find. However, luck is not on your side this time; one of the rocks you are holding onto breaks away and you tumble all the way back down to the bottom of the pit. Fortunately, the rocks beneath break your fall... as well as your spine, your limbs, and many other body parts.

GAME OVER – BETTER LUCK NEXT TIME!

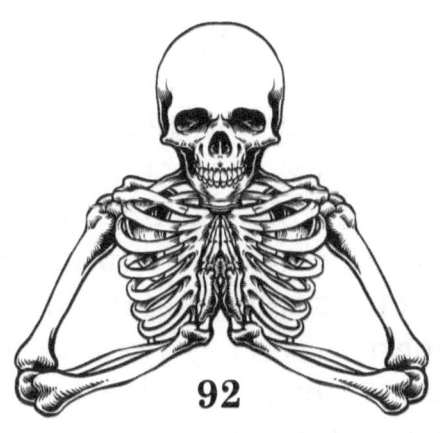

92

You stand your ground against the predator, but rather than fight it, instead you raise your hands and shout as loud as you can. The air fills with the sound of your cries, while the light filtering in through the canopy lets you cast a long, rapidly-shifting shadow. The jaguar doesn't seem scared as such, but it does reconsider whether you're worth attacking. Eventually, it decides that more easily-accessible prey is nearby, and it slinks off into the brush to find something else to devour. After the jaguar has left – and you have scanned through the foliage to make certain there aren't any other nasty surprises lying in wait – you turn your attention back towards the route to the east. With nothing else of note in the area, you decide that it would be best to keep on moving. Turn to **182**.

93

Trying to see past the tears welling up in your eyes as they are stung by the rotten air, you focus in on the finer details of the room. However, there is nothing present that you have not already discerned. This place held prisoners – be they traitors, thieves, or blasphemers – until their death. There really is nothing here for you. You move on through the corridor; turn to **48**.

94

You head towards the south, and inspect the door before you. Yet another eagle, gilded with gold, adorns its surface... but with one key difference to those that come before it: the gem in the centre. As large as a man's fist, perfectly round, and without any flaws upon its surface that you can perceive, it would certainly fetch a high price with the right buyer. But rather than feeling awe, instead you are struck by fear. A strange blue glow begins to consume you, and so too does a feeling of utter dread – one that sends a chill deep within your soul, rooting you to the spot. So great is it that you cannot even bring yourself to turn around and see the source, until it levels a blow against you – you immediately take **7** damage. When you manage to pick yourself up, and look upon your attacker, you see before you something strange, something otherworldly... something that seems, in no uncertain terms, *wrong*. It is the thing that had once seated itself upon the throne – a lich, dressed in an emperor's garb. If you wish to stand your ground and try to fight the **Lich Emperor**, turn to **154**. If you would rather flee this abomination, turn to **150**.

95

You step onto the slope, and begin to edge yourself down it a little at a time. At a few points, it feels like you're about to slip, but you manage to stabilise yourself before anything forces you to take an unwanted fall. After a while, you reach the bottom, and begin to make your way through the trees once again. To see what is past the trees, turn to **156**.

96

As you go through the door and begin to make your way along the corridor, the sound of your footsteps is quickly drowned out by the echoes of a thick stone slab slamming into the ground. A cursory examination of the slab makes it clear that there is no way back through that way – not without more powerful tools than you have at your disposal. The only thing left to do is to carry on along the corridor and attempt to be prepared for whatever it is that might come next. Turn to **100**.

97

You begin to take a closer look at various aspects of the temple's immediate interior. For the most part, there is nothing here that seems to be of any note. An academic may have been able to ascertain more about the temple, perhaps from the markings or the architecture, but there is little that you can figure out by yourself. Unable to glean anything worth remembering from the stones and dust, you instead turn your attention towards the passages to the east and west. You walk over to each one in turn, shining your flashlight into the darkness to get a better view of what they hold. As you cast light into the dark passage to the west, you see colours winding across the length and breadth of its walls. Most of it seems to have either faded with time or been washed away by water running across the stone walls, however enough of it remains that you can clearly see the corridor had once been adorned with a wide array of designs and colours, each more intricate and vibrant than the last. There are also many carvings engraved into the walls, which – though smoothed over slightly by the passage of time and erosion – are still clearly visible. In terms of its architecture, the eastern passageway is identical, standing just as tall and as wide as its western counterpart; the difference between the two is the stark lack of designs adorning this eastern corridor. It is completely barren of any paint or carvings; the closest thing that it has to any kind of decoration whatsoever are the shallow tracks left in the stone by water eroding it over the years. If you want to head down the decorated western corridor, turn to **128**. If you'd rather progress down the more barren eastern passage, turn to **185**.

98

You approach one of the walls to the side and methodically begin to scan your flashlight over it with the hope of illuminating something useful. As time wears on however, all that becomes immediately obvious is that the bricks form a pattern. The ability of the Inca stonemasons to create such a consistent size of building block may be of interest to academics studying the field, but to you it is simply an indication that you have most likely reached a dead end. Then, just as you're about to give up hope, your light reaches the edge of what seems to be a break in the pattern. Examining the wall as closely as you can, you notice that one of the blocks has a small hole dug into it – a hole that seems to be neither the result of environmental factors, nor due to something like an insect burrowing deep into the stone. Given its odd shape and depth, you surmise it must be man-made. To tap against the hole, turn to **167**. To try striking the hole with your weapon, turn to **73**. If you think it's best to return to the corridor turn to **128**. Or, if you have the **Stone Key** and think that this is the place you should use it, turn to **18**.

99

You stow your possessions deep in your pack, hoping that they won't be soaked too much by your journey through the rapids. With them safely tucked away, you take a leap into the water and it quickly becomes apparent that you were worrying over nothing. Everything you own still becomes soaked through within a matter of moments, but between the low-hanging branches slamming into you like hammers, and the sharp rocks around you acting as immovable knives, you perish long before you have the chance to care or notice.

GAME OVER – BETTER LUCK NEXT TIME!

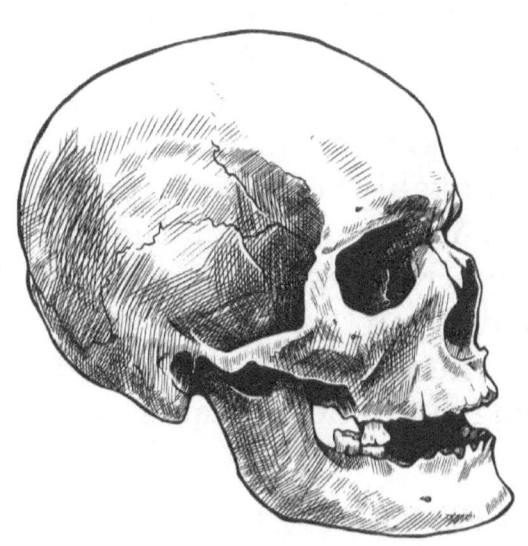

100

Your progress along the corridor is brought to an abrupt halt by it splitting into three branching paths, none of which look discernibly different from the other. The symbols carved into the stone bricks between each corridor may be some manner of clue as to which is the the path down which you should progress, but even after close examination, you cannot tell exactly what they are trying to say. Seeing no reason to linger in the area any further – and with no way back – you pick one corridor at random and head through it. After a few minutes of fumbling your way through the stone corridor, your progress is once again brought to an abrupt halt – but this time not by another split in the path; it is due to your foot sinking an inch into the floor and the unmistakable sound of a pressure plate activating. You aren't given time to hear the thunderous crashing of a stone block hitting the ground, given that it lands directly on top of you. At the very least, you can take solace in knowing your end was quick and (mostly) painless.

GAME OVER – BETTER LUCK NEXT TIME!

101

Unlike the throne room, the area you find yourself in now has no torches illuminating your surroundings. As such, you bring your flashlight back out, and scan it over the room before you, which does not seem to be the most impressive. All you can see is an assortment of shelves and racks, each containing a variety of sacks piled atop each other. There is very little to indicate that the room holds anything of material worth, though the near-perfect condition of the sacks may be of interest to an historian. Looking across the unobstructed portions of the walls, you fail to see any kind of door or anything that would indicate some kind of exit. Neither floor nor ceiling hold anything of the sort either; as far as you can tell, the only way out is the stone door at the other end of the corridor behind you, but getting past that would be impossible without the right tools. To examine the walls further, turn to **158** or to take a closer look at the sacks on the shelves, turn to **67**.

102

Deciding to heed the advice given to you by the symbol carved into the stone, you make your way through the middle door. Only moments after crossing the threshold into that corridor, a sudden crashing fills the air, and you spin on your heel to find the cause – only to see that the door behind you has been blocked off by a thick, heavy block of stone. Even a cursory examination of the object is enough to reveal that the way back is completely shut off. With the weight and strength of the block, there is no way that you could possibly move or destroy it. The only thing left to do is move forward. Turn to **200**.

103

The tunnel spits you out into yet another empty cavern, walling you in with solid grey stone. At first glance, the place appears to be nothing more than a dead end, with nothing of note for you to examine or pick up – just more rocks and rubble to ignore. Suddenly though, something lurking at the edge of your vision catches your eye, something that you somehow missed at first glance. Moving closer, you shine your flashlight on a particular section of oddly-coloured wall. Despite the stone around it being varying shades of grey, the patch itself is a kind of murky brown. This alone doesn't appear worth noting, at first – there were great stretches of stone further below that were formed from a stone of similar colour. But the pattern in this small patch isn't natural at all; the lines are too straight, too even, too consistent, the surface too flat. You deduce that it is not actually a natural formation, but is part of the temple wall – and if the draught you can feel blowing in through the gaps is any indication, then it's one that leads to a room. Given the temple's solid construction, you understand that breaking down this section of wall is a long shot, but it seems to be the only way forward. Of course, there is also the path back down; if you cannot break through the wall, you could always see if there's something you missed. If you have an item in your inventory with an attack modifier, turn to **131**. Otherwise, turn to **134**.

104

Taking a closer look at the hall reveals little that couldn't be seen with a cursory glance. It simply confirms to you that this area is as well-maintained as your initial impressions indicated. Someone – or something – has been keeping this part of the temple in near-perfect condition, with not even the slightest hint of dust or dirt present, save for what you yourself have dragged in. A shiver runs through you, and in the stillness of the room, you hear something disturbing: footsteps... and they aren't yours. The strangest thing is that they're not coming from either of the doors, nor from behind you. They're coming from *above*. Fortunately, you manage to look up just in time to see something preparing to leap down at you, and you yourself just manage to jump out of its way. Turn to **2**.

105

You emerge back into the hall, but the very moment that you do, the western door shuts behind you. A closer inspection of it reveals that, without anything powerful enough to break through it, there is no way that you are getting through. No weapon you have is strong enough to damage the stone and you certainly haven't the strength to move it aside. All that is left is to venture through the southern door. Turn to **122**.

106

Moments after entering through the door, it slams shut behind you and the familiar sound of grinding stone fills the empty air. A quick scan with your flashlight is enough to confirm that you have been locked into your current path; there is no going back now, no matter how hard you try. Turn to **20**.

107

Fortunately, the boat is light enough that you can push it out into the water and jump into it before the current pulls it away. Then, using it as a platform to jump off of, you leap with all of your strength across the water to the other half of the room. To call it a close shave is an understatement – you clear the jump by barely an inch. Anything less and you would surely have plunged into the rapids below or slipped on the wet stones and fallen to your doom. After taking one last glance behind you – and seeing that the boat has long since vanished into the abyss – you begin the walk towards the heavy door you sighted earlier. Turn to **86**.

108

Climbing onto the trunk proves to be difficult, given the lack of footholds. Moreover, the water has left the few that are available so slick that maintaining a secure hold on them proves to be a difficult task to manage. It isn't impossible though, and you eventually manage to clamber onto the very top, where the wet surfaces are of the least concern. However, despite taking this precaution, it does not avail you. The trunk, though it looked solid, is actually rotten and brittle. No sooner do you take one step forwards, you fall straight through it, with the force of the drop enough to carry you through the bottom as well. At least your end is quick – even if being torn to ribbons by the current and jagged stones is far from painless.

GAME OVER – BETTER LUCK NEXT TIME!

109

Your attention turns towards the spot in the wall you believe is weak. It's a long shot, but it's all you've got to go on right now. Then, with frantic energy driven by adrenaline, you begin to throw yourself against the wall. Your efforts at first seem to be in vain, but the faint crumbling you hear is all you need for you to redouble your efforts. That, and the footsteps growing ever closer to your position. Eventually, after what feels like an age, you manage to put enough force into just the right area and part of the wall comes crashing down. The bricks topple through... but you neither hear the crash of them landing, nor do you see them hit the ground. When you peer past the gap you've made, you see why, as what lies beyond the wall isn't a stretch of cave or yet another corridor... it's a yawning chasm, so dark that you cannot see the bottom of it from your position. Turning around to check behind you, you see the door has already been opened, and undead warriors are filtering through it at an alarming pace. You carefully weigh up your chances of jumping versus turning back and trying to run past the foes that are present in the room, and realise that neither option is particularly welcoming. If you think there's something in turning to face the way you came and trying to run past the warriors before they realise what's going on, turn to **70**. If instead you fancy your chances down in the pit, turn to **3**.

110

You take as many steps back as the limited space allows you to and steel yourself for the jump ahead. Then, with every fibre of strength in your body, you take a running leap across the river, letting out a primal roar. None hear this impressive cry, however – nor do they hear the pathetic screams that follow as you realise that the river is simply too wide for you to make it across. In an instant, the rapids seems to reach up and take hold of you, before unceremoniously slamming you into every piece of rock and wood that it can reach. Needless to say, you do not survive this barrage, and it is not long before the water washes away the very last trace of your blood from the rocks.

GAME OVER – BETTER LUCK NEXT TIME!

111

Shortly after continuing west, you reach a wooden door that – like the rest of the temple before it – seems almost entirely unused. As it slowly creaks open, you peer past the threshold and see a large room decorated with... nothing. As far as you can tell, the floor is bare slabs of stone laid next to each other, while the walls are the same but in a vertical manner. Regardless of where you shine your flashlight, the room seems to hold nothing but dust and dirt, with the only sign of either having been disturbed being the droplets of condensation that slide down the wall once every so often. If you think the room may still hold a secret, turn to **98**. Otherwise, turn to **128** to return to the corridor.

112

No sooner do you cross over into the middle corridor than it is blocked off by a stone slab. With it being too heavy to move, and no way to make it retract back into the wall, it becomes apparent that you are now locked into the path that you have chosen. Turn to **141**.

113

You begin to move towards the throne, stepping ever closer with your eyes fixed upon its lustrous golden glow. Its allure beckons like the singing of a siren calling you towards fathomless wealth. But alongside the tantalising prospect of riches beyond your wildest dreams comes a chill in the air – one that seems to cut deep into you, striking to the very core of your being. Even with the throne in reach, you cannot shake the feeling of growing dread; it gnaws at you from deep within, its grip growing tighter until you are no more than a metre from the golden structure. There, almost within arm's reach of the throne, the underlying terror reaches its zenith and the cause is revealed. It is not magic cast upon the throne, nor the room itself – it is the figure you now see sitting upon it. What at first appears to be the skeletal remains of a human begin to stir, and a pale blue glow grows brighter in each eye. Stricken by fear, you step backwards, your every instinct screaming at you to flee from this otherworldly threat. And yet, your legs remain still, your body trembling at the mere sight of the figure rising. But despite it all, you remain composed enough at least to glance to the side, and see tendrils of blue light stretching towards the living corpse, sinking deep into it. It is then that you realise the fate of all those that had come before you. Lining the walls to either side of the throne are the bodies of explorers from throughout the centuries, from Spanish conquerors of ages past to bold adventurers who once could have been your peers. Their bodies, though made pale by death's cold grip, appear perfectly preserved – but this does not last for long. The figure's magic seems to drain them, and in moments they are no more than dust and damaged clothing. Your gaze turns back towards the thing that had been in the throne, and only then do you realise what it truly is. Garbed in brightly-dyed clothing, the beast before you is no mere corpse – it is a **Lich**, preserved by the unholy grip of undeath. To fight the **Lich Emperor**, turn to **154**, or to turn tail and run turn to **150**.

114

Wanting to get a better idea of your surroundings, you begin to examine the area around you, attempting to discern anything interesting. Though someone of a more scholarly stripe might have something to say about the immediate environment, you yourself see little of note. It is only when you get ready to move on that you see something out of the corner of your eye that seems off; you turn and crouch to take a closer look at what at first appears to be just a depression in the dirt. However, a more thorough examination reveals it to be the tracks of some big cat or other. It seems that it's a fresh print too. The sight immediately puts you on guard and not a moment too soon. Something enormous leaps out of the shadows, its sights firmly set on you. You only just manage to dive out of the way and when you finally do lock eyes with your attacker, you see exactly what created those prints: it's a **Jaguar** – and not a friendly one either. If you choose to fight the beast, turn to **41**. If you think you might be able to scare it away, turn to **92**. Or, if terror has gotten the better of you and you think the best option is to run, turn to **30**.

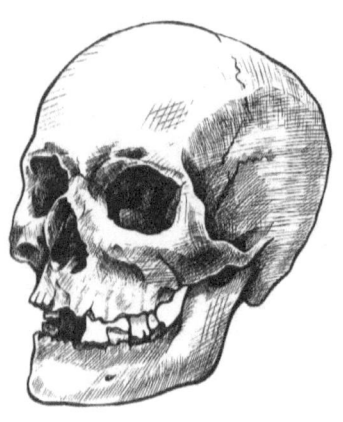

115

You turn towards the nearest rock and with the few seconds you have left on the ledge, you jump towards it. Your hands only just find the edge and against all odds you manage to grip onto it. Unfortunately, your dangling body is soon enveloped by the sand below, which seems to add more and more weight to your body. You try so hard to pull yourself up onto the rock but you just don't have the strength. Soon, your grip fails and your final moments are spent thinking about how despite each breath you take is becoming smaller and smaller, the pain of the sand entering your lungs gets ever worse, right up to the point of death.

GAME OVER – BETTER LUCK NEXT TIME!

116

Wandering about the sandy cavern, you begin to examine the environment much more thoroughly. You don't see much that you couldn't already make out from the entrance. None of the rocks – nor the sand itself – seem to hold anything of value. However, you do notice that the pit contains a few rocks jutting up out of the shifting sands. Given how many there are, and the pattern they are arranged in, there's a chance that you could use them as platforms to jump across. On the other hand, you can see a ledge stretching around the edge of the pit. Jutting out from the wall, it connects both sides of the cavern, and seems as though it might be just wide enough for you to squeeze across. If you want to take a running leap across the pit, turn to **28**, or to attempt a series of smaller jumps using the rocks turn to **34**. If you think that sidling around the edge is the best option, turn to **23**.

117

Finally, you emerge out of the winding tunnel, and shine your flashlight upon the area before you. It is, for the most part, just damp stone: some smooth, some craggy, some jagged, but all just stone. However, cutting through the middle of the room, like a cleaver slicing the stone apart, is an underground river. Frothing white with the force of the current carrying the water deeper into the Earth, the roar that echoes off the stone is like thunder, almost deafening to behold. Even from the distance at which you are standing, you can feel the force behind the torrent. To examine the area further, turn to **19**, or to jump across the river, turn to **9**.

118

With what little time is left, you crouch, then spring off towards solid ground. You come close... but not close enough. The jump is just enough to allow your fingertips to graze against the rock, but you cannot get a solid grip on it. You find yourself sinking into the sand that grips your entire body, dragging you down slowly, and giving you ample time to contemplate your mistakes before inhaling your final, sandy breath.

GAME OVER – BETTER LUCK NEXT TIME!

119

The corridor's exit deposits you into another hall – though this time, you can actually see the ceiling. What truly sets it apart from the gargantuan space behind you is the sheer number of eagle statues that are arranged against either wall. Each faces a different direction, standing upon a giant stone platform, watching over the room like a silent guardian. To examine the area further, turn to **78**, or to continue moving swiftly down the hall, turn to **166**.

120

Rather than risk your life against the giant mass of clay and gemstones, you decide instead to flee down the corridor. Despite the statue's apparent strength, it is as heavy and lumbering as it looks and struggles even to turn in time to see you run down the corridor. A quick glance back confirms that even were it fast enough to give chase, its body is far too large to allow it through the entrance. For now, you are safe, and can instead focus on making your way through the rest of the temple. To progress, turn to **57**.

121

As deadly a predator as the jaguar was, you finally manage to prevail, defending yourself successfully against the beast. After a hard-fought battle it lies still against the forest floor and you are finally left in peace. All that is left is to keep going down the path that you have chosen. To keep moving through the jungle, turn to **182**.

122

Only a moment after you step into the southern passage, the door drops loudly into place behind you; thankfully it did not crush you, but there seems to be no obvious mechanism to open it again. Banging repeatedly on the stone achieves nothing, and it is clear from just a glance that it is far too heavy for you to lift up or break through. The only thing left to do is to keep moving south, which is exactly what you do. As you take in the path ahead, you note that the corridor itself is a far cry from those that came before it. The stone, for starters, is in a far better state than what you have seen previously. Appearing brand new and polished, not a single inch of it shows signs of wear or tear. Not a drop of water nor stray weed can be seen on its surface or even between the slabs; the only 'detriments' to the stonework's perfect smoothness are the geometric carvings etched regularly along the walls, each inlaid with glistering gold. When you first looked into the corridor it was dark, but now it is fully lit by torches lining the walls each side of you; somehow, they ignite when you are within a certain distance, bathing the area in a dazzling brightness that causes the gold to glimmer almost blindingly. It is certainly a far grander affair than the corridors before – though whether this is a good or bad sign remains to be seen. To proceed further south, turn to **194**.

123

After looking around to find a point from which to descend from the ledge, you see a slope leading towards the lower ground. Though it doesn't let you climb down, you are at least able to slide down it without too much issue, besides the addition of grass stains to your clothing. This isn't of much concern to you, however – it's far from the worst thing that's gotten on them during your journey through the jungle. To take stock of the lower ground on which you now stand, turn to **46**.

124

The **Clay Guardian**'s strength overwhelms you, and you are rendered incapable of so much as swinging a fist against it. The last thing you see before you succumb to your injuries is the living statue picking you up by your ankle and dragging you off into the temple depths for a purpose you will never know.

GAME OVER – BETTER LUCK NEXT TIME!

125

Within the first few steps of you making your way southwards, an awful feeling washes over you; the shiver of someone walking over your grave. At first you continue trudging along, but soon you come to a halt and make a decision. You cannot explain exactly why you turn around, but after you do, you are absolutely sure that something is watching you from the darkness. You begin to run back the way you came and as you approach the place where the passage split, you dare to look behind you, only to see... nothing. Not looking where you are going, you trip over a stone on the ground that is raised slightly higher than the others and end up head first in a pool of water. Turn to **25**.

126

Using your **Machete** both to chop away broad sections of the tree and to hack off vines for use as ropes and fastenings, you manage create a raft. Though it doesn't feel especially sturdy, you are particularly pleased with your handiwork as – in your opinion, at least – it seems solid enough for you to use it to cross over to the other side of the stream. You push the craft out onto the water and jump onboard, using a long branch to steer towards the opposite bank. Sadly, your crafting skills aren't as good as you had at first though, and the raft begins to break apart, its bindings snapping and untying at an alarming rate. With barely a few seconds left before the whole thing sinks, you make a decision to leap to safety – but which way? To jump towards the nearest rock, turn to **129**, or to attempt the long leap towards the bank you were originally trying to reach, turn to **66**.

127

You inspect the pit that surrounds you, but manage to discern little of note. It is, quite simply, a dark pit: nothing more, nothing less. Remarkably, it seems your pursuers haven't followed... but the reason is unclear. Perhaps their magic binds them to the temple? Maybe they knew better than to jump in after you? Or was their goal simply to drive you off rather than actually kill you? It's difficult to say, and as you need to be on your guard, it's best not to spend too long pondering things. You strain your ears in the hope of detecting whether there is anything particularly dangerous down either path, and can hear two distinct noises. To the south, there is the sound of running water – a river, perhaps? It's impossible to tell at this point what the water source is, but one would assume it isn't stagnant. Meanwhile, to the west you can make out the sound of crumbling rock and shifting stone, but not like the doors above; here, it sounds natural, as if parts of the wall are simply falling away over time. It's time to make your choice. To head south towards the water, turn to **180**, or to investigate the more earthy sounds to the west, turn to **168**.

128

Turning towards the western corridor, you start to walk again, your ever-trusty flashlight illuminating the path before you. Besides the steady dripping of water, your footsteps are the only thing that make noise; with your senses on overdrive, their sound seems to echo out for miles both behind and ahead of you. For a while, it seems that this narrow stretch is all that there is to see, but eventually you begin to see openings either side of you. There is one to the north, and one to the south, though you cannot tell where either leads without moving closer. To examine the area further, turn to **55**. To head through the northern opening, turn to **5**, or turn to **136** for the southern passage. If none of these options appeal to you, the only choice left is to continue heading west, in which case you should turn to **111**.

129

Just as the last vestiges of your raft begin to sink, you make the leap towards the rocks jutting out above the stream's surface. Sadly, this proves to be a fatal mistake. The rocks are far too slick for you to get a hold on, and though you manage to stay alive for all of a few seconds, the heavy currents soon rip you away from safety, pulling you down to a watery grave in no time at all.

GAME OVER – BETTER LUCK NEXT TIME!

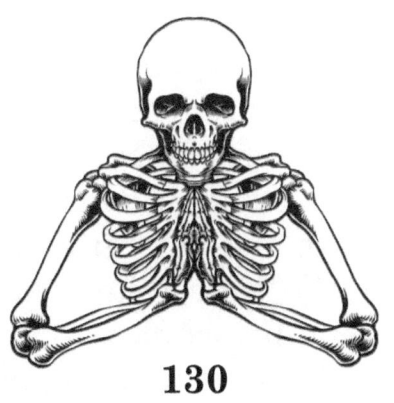

130

As you emerge from the previous area's death-ridden confines, you find yourself in a significantly smaller – and emptier – room than before. There is nothing in the way of decoration, though thankfully this also means a lack of centuries-old human remains to lend a macabre air to the place. The only thing of note is the presence of three doors at the end of the room. With any possible exit behind you blocked off, you'll need to choose one of these. If you wish to go through the door to your left, turn to **16**. To go through the one to your right, turn to **63**. If you'd rather try the central door, turn to **32**.

131

Using your weapon, you begin to strike at the wall. Though your previous experiences have demonstrated the sturdiness of the structure, this particular section seems to have been damaged enough by the wear and tear of time that there is the tiniest hint of give to the bricks. Summoning what strength you still can, you pound and smash against the wall with all your might, and not a moment too soon one of the giant stones crumbles apart, revealing a small gap. It's a tight squeeze, but it looks like you'll be able to get through it. To see what awaits you on the other side, turn to **44**.

132

As you enter the temple and shine your flashlight over the scene before you, it soon becomes apparent that you are the first living soul to have set foot in this temple for years. Upon every surface is a thick layer of dust and dirt, surely undisturbed for centuries. The only signs of life seem to be the cobwebs lingering in the corners, though most of these are covered in dust and look to have been long since abandoned by their inhabitants. There hangs a dank, musty smell, its rank odour as thick as tar – clearly even fresh air has eluded this place. As you sweep the beam around, you take note of two passageways leading away from this entry room: one to the east, and one to the west. Neither are lit however, and you can hear nothing more than the quiet dripping of condensation coming from both. To examine this entryway further, turn to **97**. To head off east, turn to **185**. Or to set off down the western passageway, turn to **128**.

133

You carefully examine the ledge to see what options lay before you. Behind you is the path from which you came, and at first it looks like your only option is to turn back and head that way. But a closer look reveals a slope leading down towards a section of the rainforest below. Though climbing back up might be difficult, scaling down shouldn't be a problem; you suspect the worst thing that could happen to you would be a scraped knee. To head down the slope, turn to **95**. Or, if you think it looks a little too risky for your liking, head back the way you came and turn to **16**.

134

You slam your foot against the wall, and repeatedly throw your weight against it, but nothing comes of your efforts. There simply isn't enough give in the masonry for you to break through and make your way to the other side. With no other path forward available, your only option is to make your way back down towards the lower level of the cavern network. Turn to **145**.

135

As you emerge into the next room, it becomes immediately apparent where the path has led you. Past aging stone pillars as tall and wide as the mighty trees outside, you can see am underground river cutting through the stone floor in the distance. It divides the room in half like a knife, while its rushing waters lead off into yet another murky expanse.

Past the opposite bank, you can see that yet more stone slabs are laid upon the ground – most likely leading to another section of the temple. To examine the area further, turn to **29**. If you want to try and jump across to the other side of the room, turn to **110**. Or, to enter the water and swim downriver, turn to **99**.

136

The door opens to reveal what surely used to be an armoury full of weapons; some are sitting on racks, some hung upon hooks.

Slings, bows and arrows, axes, clubs, shields, and spears fill the area, leaving little more than scant glimpses of the walls. However, the majority of the weapons have been rendered useless due to their age; wood has rotted away rendering handles broken and brittle, bowstrings are near nonexistent, having withered away into nothing but a few short threads, slings are little more than frayed fabric, incapable of flinging much more than the dust settling upon them and the blades you can see are so dull they'd struggle to cut into a pound of butter. Despite your suspicion that there's nothing useful in this room, you could take another riffle through the racks – turn to **161** if you think this is worthwhile. If you're keen to get moving on the other hand, turn to **128**.

137

You tread slowly forwards, placing each step only after careful consideration. The approach works, but only for a time. You manage to avoid slipping off, but the tree is not stable enough to remain in place – and no amount of well-balanced steps is enough to keep it from falling into the stream, taking you with it. Your fortune seems to take a shift for the better – for a moment – when it appears that the tree will block you from getting dashed against the rocks – only for your head to slam directly against its hardest part, knocking you unconscious and thus drowning you rather spectacularly beneath the foam.

GAME OVER – BETTER LUCK NEXT TIME!

138

As interesting as the patterns may be, they are of absolutely no use to you, and they pale into insignificance when compared to the item you now see resting upon a stone plinth: a **Golden Dagger** beset with beautiful jewels, its every inch glistening in the light cast upon it. Based upon your knowledge of ancient societies, you surmise that it must be an ornamental – or more likely ceremonial piece. The metal is too soft to be of any use in battle, and even if it were stronger, the shape of the blade would make it impractical regardless. The one thing about it you are absolutely certain of is that it will fetch a high price on the antiques market, and even if this weren't the case, the value of the metal and gemstones will see you living comfortably for many a year... *if* you make it out of here alive, of course.

ITEM AVAILABLE

Golden Dagger: Though not of much use in a fight, the materials from which the dagger is made are sure to fetch a small fortune.

Whether you choose to take the dagger with you or leave it behind, you need to get moving. To carry on the way you were headed, turn to **51**. Or, if you suspect that there is something you might have missed in the areas you have previously explored, turn to **65**.

139

You analyse the next leap, making similar estimations of the distance, the angle, the amount of rebound you expect and so on. Confidently you launch yourself towards your target and... prove that your previous success was merely luck as you land nowhere near the point you thought you would, suffocating to death in the sand in a matter of seconds.

GAME OVER – BETTER LUCK NEXT TIME!

140

Your efforts to overcome the big cat fail, and you succumb to its superior strength and speed. The last thing that you are conscious of is it tearing you apart – but at least the beast has had the courtesy to give you some precious seconds to realise how bad of an idea fighting a jaguar actually is.

GAME OVER – BETTER LUCK NEXT TIME!

141

As you trudge down the corridor, you come upon a path that splits three ways, each path having a symbol etched into the ground before it. With no reference to what the symbol means however, you cannot discern what the marks are meant to convey. All you can do therefore is choose a path at random. Soon you come to yet another similar junction, then another. Your journey through the maze ends a few minutes later; not due to reaching its exit point, but because you step upon a pressure plate, which activates a storm of poisoned darts. Around a dozen tiny projectiles pierce your skin and your vision begins to fade as you crumple into a heap on the floor. The one small mercy afforded to you is that the temple's architects at least had the courtesy to include a numbing agent with the toxicant so that you feel no pain as your internals organs shut down one by one.

GAME OVER – BETTER LUCK NEXT TIME!

142

The path upwards is in fact a hole in the ceiling, into which you shine your flashlight to see if there is anything either of interest or to be avoided. Unsurprisingly, your light does not reach all the way through the darkness, plaguing the potential way forward; you will have to climb up to figure out what it hides. At least the walls seem to have plenty of footholds, crimps and nooks to assist your climb, though whether they'll hold out long enough for you to make full use of them or crumble in the middle of your ascent is another question entirely. If you want to give it a go, turn to **31**. Or, to investigate the route downwards, turn to **171**.

143

As you head southwards, the trees begin to thin out until only a few are left either side. At first you consider this to be a fortunate turn of events, but soon the reason for their sparsity becomes clear — there's nothing for any such flora in which to take root. The path ends most abruptly, leading only to a steep drop downwards from a rocky ledge. With no way to scale it safely, your only options are to backtrack completely, or take the western path at the previous junction. To head back, turn to **16** or to make your way west, turn to **77**.

144

You pace over to the western door, and inspect it carefully, hoping to find anything that could shed light on how you should progress, but sadly there are no symbols carved into the stone to direct you. What you can perceive, however, is the faint sound of footsteps coming from somewhere above you. Before you have a chance to process this information, the entity making the sounds crashes down behind you, striking its weapon hard against your back. Take **5** damage and turn to **2**.

145

With the wall in front of you being such a solid, sturdy and unbreakable barrier, you decide to make your way back down to the lower levels. Though delving even deeper into the caverns feels like the wrong direction in which to head, it really is the only option you can take at this point. To start climbing down, turn to **68**.

146

As you approach the corridor, you think you see something move out of the corner of your eye. Quickly, you sweep the beam of the flashlight towards the area you think it came from... but you see nothing; no rat scurrying away from you, no wayward lizard creeping through the darkness. You shake your head and once again – though a little more cautiously now

— you take a few steps forward. There again, the movement! One more time however, all you illuminate is fungi and dank cavern walls. There's definitely something off about all of this. If you want to continue approaching the corridor confidently along your current path, turn to **160**. If you want to check out a particularly large cluster of fungi that you have just noticed, turn to **17**. If inspecting the statue is your priority, turn to **155**, or to check out the patterns carved into the bricks a little more closely, turn to **40**.

147

Although impressive, the statues aren't designed to help you find your way. It is, in fact, a small slab on the floor by the middle passage which is the temple architect's indication of which route the smart explorer should follow. The question is, do you trust them? If you think the **Notes** that you have taken have a solid foundation, turn to **102**. If your gut feeling is telling you to take the left door however, turn to **172**. Finally, if 'right is right' happens to be one of your maxims, turn to **175**.

148

You trek along endless corridors, each one branching many times. It's clear that you are in the middle of a maze, and you realise that your key task is to figure out a way to reach the exit – or at least get back to where you came from. At the next junction, you note a carving on the floor that appears similar to the ones you have noted down. Closer inspection reveals it to be almost identical – and the few differences can be chalked up to imprecisions in your sketching. After examining it, you determine the path you should be following and proceed onwards confidently. Turn to **58**.

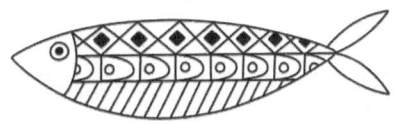

149

Having risen to your feet, it seems that the mud in which you currently stand is thigh-deep. Though it slows you down significantly, requiring a herculean level of effort to take each step, you are still able to force yourself forward, but the hard slog becomes exponentially more difficult once branching paths become more and more common. The strange markings on the walls do not help either, given that they do not match any knowledge you have of the Inca civilisation. Your only option is to continue your struggle along the current path. Turn to **71**.

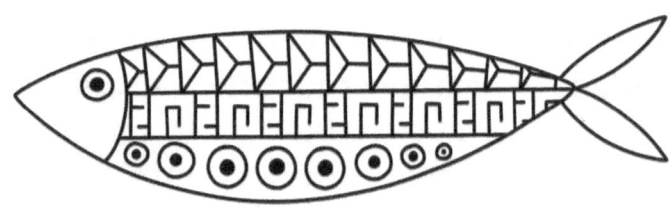

150

Unwilling to pit yourself against an undead wielder of magic beyond your understanding, you break towards the southern door to try and escape its clutches. You manage to reach the entryway before the otherworldly enemy can catch you, but you see no mechanism by which to open the door nor will brute force be of any help. You must think quickly; the **Lich Emperor** is closing in, and its gaze is firmly set upon you. If you have a **Mysterious Blue Gem**, turn to **173**, or if not, turn to **26**.

151

The corridor is filled by nothing but dirt, dust and deathly silence. Every movement you make – from your steps forward even to the slightest twitch of your muscles – is enough to send echoes reverberating up and down the passageway until they eventually fade into nothingness. The sense of dread that lingers in the air does not abate when the beam of your flashlight reveals another room – in fact, for some reason it only grows more intense. To venture into the room, turn to **81**

152

You take in your surroundings and note that apart from the stream, the entire area around you appears to be the jungle to which you have become accustomed. Trees reach high into the air, shrouding the ground blow in darkness via their thick canopy of leaves. Numerous fauna are scurrying about, eyeing you suspiciously; flora of every shape and size take up what little space is left between the trees. You could try and jump across the stream, in which case you should turn to **13**. Alternatively, you might risk climbing down from the ledge, a path which – now you can see it clearly – does seem a little steep; for this option, turn to **123**.

153

Deciding not to take the risk of falling into the water along with the bridge, you hurry across the last stretch. As if in mocking response, the trunk shakes just enough to send you tumbling downwards – but with *just* enough momentum that, instead of hitting the water, you slam hard against the ground. Despite the pain of falling on solid stone, you take solace in the fact that you weren't swept away with the tree, which is now tumbling down the stream to who-knows-where. All that is left now is to keep moving through the jungle in your search for the path to the temple. Turn to **182**.

154

What stands before you is no mere zombie, nor is it some shambling, mindless corpse. It is an unholy abomination, tethered to the living realm by the darkest of arcane arts. Its skin and flesh have long since rotted away, and yet its bones move with more strength and purpose than any living person. Its only weapon seems to be the staff gripped in its hand, and yet it radiates power that shakes you to your core more than any modern man or weapon could ever hope to. It has no eyes, and yet the pale blue light that resides within its skull pierces you with more ferocity than any gaze you have known. A glance alone is enough to assure you of this thing's strength, even though you are sure you've only felt a fraction of what it is truly capable of.

Lich Emperor
HP: 25
Attack: 9
Defence: 6

ENEMY ENCOUNTER

If you win the fight, turn to **10**, or if you are defeated, turn to **202**.

155

You shine your flashlight directly at the statue and examine it closely. In stark contrast to the artefacts above ground, it appears to have been moved recently... or, worryingly, *maintained*. Whether the lack of dust is due to the river's spray washing it off or not is one thing, but the patterns carved into it that have clearly been made recently is another altogether, and the gems used as eyes have been polished by someone (or some*thing)* to a flawless mirror gleam. As you examine the statue, your worst fears are realised; it begins to shake then moves towards you, raising its arms in readiness to strike. Fortunately, it is slow and lumbering and you dodge its first hit without issue. If you want to stay and fight, turn to **88**. Or, to turn tail and run, go to **120**.

156

Within a few minutes of passing the trees, you feel a sharp pain in your ankle and look down to see the cause. You note two puncture wounds in your ankle and immediately spot a long, thin shape slithering away. Too late do you realise that there was a snake hidden in the shadows, and before you have a chance to dig through your pack to search for the appropriate anti-venom, your extremities become numb. Your limbs follow shortly after, followed by the rest of your body. Sapped of strength, you now cannot even lift your head, and as the powerful toxin reaches your heart, you spend your final, agonising moments wishing you had taken better precautions.

GAME OVER – BETTER LUCK NEXT TIME!

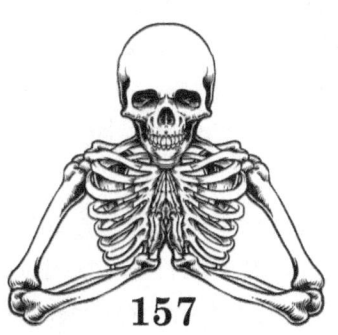

157

Finally, the tunnel opens up, but only to reveal yet more stone. This room, however, seems mercifully free of traps or bottomless sandy pits. It does make up for it though by having another fork in the path; there is one way leading upwards and another straight down. To examine the former, turn to **142**. For the latter, turn to **171**.

158

A closer look at the walls reveals little, at first. The brickwork seems solid and well-maintained, to the point where not even time has managed to cause any major hints of wear or tear. But as you focus, you can feel a draught coming from the south. It is faint, but there is just enough of a disturbance in the air to follow it to a spot on the wall. Pushing against the bricks from behind which the breeze is coming, you can feel the slightest amount of give. It is only a little, but with enough force, you might be able to knock down this part of the wall... and if the draught is anything to go by, it could mean that you're able to escape from the treasury. Before you have a chance to test your theory however, you hear something in the distance, echoing off the walls of the corridor: footsteps – and far more than just one person's. Even if you were to have the greatest of luck on your side, you figure your chances of fending off more than one of the undead at a time are slim at best, and that perhaps it would be best to retreat instead of stand and fight. However, with so many soldiers, somewhere around here there's surely treasure to match.

To take a closer look at the sacks, turn to **24**. If preparing to fight the incoming horde is your priority, turn to **199**. Or, to try and break down the wall, turn to **19**.

159

Whilst you are surrounded by a king's ransom in treasure, it is worth nothing if you cannot escape from your confines. However, as fortune would have it, the defeat of the **Golden Guardian** seems to have triggered some other arcane mechanism within the temple. At the opposite end of the room, a previously smooth section of the wall retracts to the side, and reveals yet another dark passageway beyond. There is no way of telling what lies beyond – no sound, no sight nor even smell. As foreboding as this is, however, there is no way back; you have absolutely no choice but to press onwards. Turn to **151**.

160

Deciding to ignore your gut suspicions, you focus your light on the corridor entrance, once again walking towards it. No sooner do you take the first step than you hear the sound of grinding stone and another set of footfalls behind you. Swiftly, you turn around to see what is causing the noise – but you are not nearly swift enough, for the statue that had been standing to the entrance's side has come to life and already dealt a heavy blow against you: take **4** damage. To stand your ground and fight, turn to **88**, or to run like a coward, turn to **120**.

161

As you begin to look around, at first it seems that your suspicions are correct: there is little in the room that could prove useful, if anything. However, as you examine the array of decayed weapons a little more closely, you notice that a few pieces still seem to be intact enough that you could use them. It is doubtful that they would survive much punishment, but should anyone or anything prove hostile, they are a better option than your bare hands. Amongst the racks is also a small selection of shields that while perhaps not quite as sturdy as something crafted in the modern era, are still solid enough to work with.

ITEMS AVAILABLE

Mace: A length of wood with a heavy piece of metal attached to the end. **+3** to attack rolls.

Spear: A wooden pole, with a sharp piece of metal at one end. **+5** to attack rolls, but takes up two inventory slots.

Small Shield: A square shield made of wood. **-1** to enemy attack rolls.

Large Shield: A rectangular shield made of wood. **-3** to enemy attack rolls, but takes up two inventory slots.

Once you have chosen which items to bring with you – if any – you resume your trek. Turn to **128**.

162

Though the fire around the statuette causes you to hesitate, ultimately you decide that the gem inside has to be worth the risk. Amazingly, reaching into the alcove proves your fears to be unfounded; rather than causing you to flinch back in pain, the flames are instead just pleasantly warm. With the risk of burning yourself eliminated, you remove the hammer and chisel from your backpack and slowly begin to chip away at the stone holding the gem in place. Working with the glare of the flames directly in your eyes proves difficult, but ultimately manageable. Eventually you manage to create something of a gap around the gem, which you pry loose with the chisel. Immediately following its removal, there is a loud – almost deafening – grinding cacophony of stone grinding slowly against stone. Like the panel that revealed the alcove, another part of the wall in front of you begins to give way – though this time, on a far larger scale. Slowly, inch by inch, an entire block of the wall sinks into the floor, revealing beyond it a passageway. Past the threshold is a flight of stone steps, each one leading further and further down into the darkness, reaching so far that not even your flashlight can see to the bottom. Though you cannot see to the ultimate depths, straining your ears allows you to hear the sound of rushing water in the distance, like a rapidly flowing river.

ITEM AVAILABLE

Mysterious Blue Gem: A small oval-shaped gem that appears to be some kind of sapphire, though only an expert would know for certain.

To traverse down the stairs, turn to **87**.

163

As is typical of a maze, more branching paths stand in your way – and at every one, the symbol carved into the floor steers you towards a single path from the three available. For a while, you believe yourself to be going in the correct direction... right up until the moment a barrage of poison darts is fired directly at your face. Though the agony of at least three of the projectiles penetrating your eyeballs is immense, you take some comfort knowing this brings the relief of death just a little quicker.

GAME OVER – BETTER LUCK NEXT TIME!

164

You cast your light down the corridor, and begin the journey towards whatever lays beyond the avian stone sentinels. The passageway you are walking through is rather plain, with the only thing of note being a pattern incorporating eagles facing in various directions running through the middle of the walls on either side of you. To enter the room at the end, turn to **119**.

165

After carefully weighing your options, you decide upon the ingenious idea of plunging headfirst into rapids moving fast enough to rip a man to shreds in seconds. Miraculously, your dip in the stream does not result in your bones being reduced to a fine powder. Not so miraculously, the enormous school of violent, carnivorous fish below the surface immediately rush to tear you apart.

GAME OVER – BETTER LUCK NEXT TIME!

166

You hurry down the middle of the hall towards the door. Although normally you would pace yourself, the thought of having to fend off or run from a swarm of eagles is bad enough – never mind stone ones. Even when you manage to make it past the point where the eagles could fit into the corridor, you glance over your shoulder once or twice, wanting to be absolutely certain that you are safe from them. To see what lays beyond the eagle-lined hall, turn to **50**.

167

You rap your knuckles sharply against the hole, and listen closely to the sound it makes. Though it is faint, you can just about hear that the space behind the hole is empty – though, pressing your eye up against it, the hole is too narrow and too dark to see what might be beyond it. To try striking the hole with your weapon, turn to **73**. If you think it's best to return to the corridor turn to **128**. Or, if you have the **Stone Key** and think that this is the place you should use it, turn to **18**.

168

You decide on the western path and slowly begin to make your way forwards, flashlight scanning every surface on the lookout for anything dangerous. As you venture deeper in, your footsteps are accompanied by a faint crunching, which grows louder the further in you move. A quick inspection of the ground reveals the cause to be sand – a thin carpet of it, growing thicker with every step. To discover where the sand is coming from, turn to **35**.

169

As if the hall itself has recognised your victory, the southern door begins to rumble, sending out a thunderous booming noise. You expect it to sink into the floor, but in fact it begins to recede into the ceiling instead, rising gradually until there is room enough for you to pass. The path unveiled is cloaked in darkness; seeing what is beyond would take a stronger light than you have. The only way to find out what lies to the south is to see for yourself – turn to **122**.

170

You reach out towards the statuette, despite having more than a little hesitation due the fire surrounding it. While holding the head with one hand, you attempt to wrench the gem free with the other – and amazingly find that the flames, despite their glow, do not burn you; in fact, they're pleasantly warm. As for the gem you are attempting to grab, it is set firmly into the stone, and does not prove easy to pry loose. No matter how hard you pull, it remains firmly in place, budging not even a fraction of an inch. You keep trying nonetheless and finally it does begin to shift – along with the rest of the statuette. Though the stone does not come loose, the statuette it is attached to leans towards you, revealing the fact that the entire thing is an elaborate lever... but you are not given the time to appreciate this. In an instant, you are blinded by a brilliant flash of searing orange light, having just enough time to realise that it is the fire flaring up and filling the room entirely. In less than a second, the bright glow has disappeared, but only because your eyeballs have melted. By this point you are completely consumed by the flames, the gentle warmth having transformed into an immolating funeral pyre. The sole remaining mercy is that the fire is hot enough to reduce you to a pile of ashes in only seconds. Your death, though painful, is at least quick.

GAME OVER – BETTER LUCK NEXT TIME!

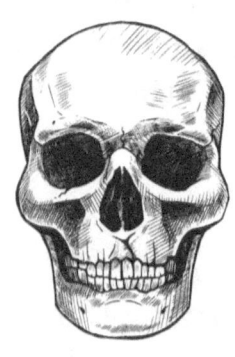

171

Standing at the edge of the hole, you shine your light in trying to see its depths, though doing so reveals little; it is far too dark and deep, and it seems the only way you'll get information on it is by climbing down. At least the walls seem to have plenty of footholds and crevices that you can step onto and leverage yourself against. If you want to proceed downwards, turn to **68**. Or, to take stock and investigate the path leading upwards a little more, turn to **142**.

172

Despite the symbol on the floor indicating that the middle path is the correct one, you decide to head down the left path instead. You do not get a chance to change your mind about this, as the second that you cross into the left corridor, the doorway is blocked off by a dense stone slab. A brief investigation reveals that it is far too strong for you to break and far too heavy to move. You have no choice but to progress down the path that you have chosen. Turn to **36**.

173

A flash of inspiration hits you and you hold the blue gem in your possession up next to the similar one on the door. Both glow faintly and after a second passes, the door begins to slide into the ceiling. You don't even wait for it to open fully; as soon as there is enough of a gap for you to throw yourself through, you scramble into the corridor beyond, and attempt to leave the **Lich Emperor** behind. To take stock of where you are, turn to **45**.

174

You delve into the path set out before you, but as it splits into three corridors, you realise it is actually a maze. With no map to guide you, you wander aimlessly for a while and it is not long before you find yourself hopelessly lost within the labyrinth's stone confines. Fortunately, you are spared from a slow and agonising death from starvation. Unfortunately, it is because you trigger a concealed pressure plate, falling painfully into a spike pit deep beneath the ground.

GAME OVER – BETTER LUCK NEXT TIME!

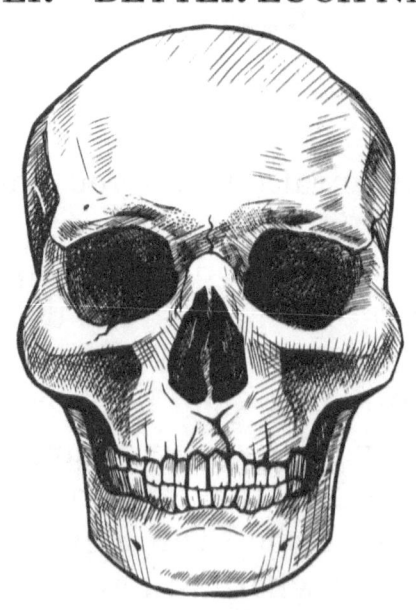

175

Despite the indicator pointing out the middle entrance, you elect instead to head down the right-hand path instead. This is not a decision that you can take back, as the very second you pass through the wooden doorway, a stone slab falls heavily into place behind you. With neither the strength nor tools to move or destroy it, you are left with only one option: to move forward down the corridor that you have chosen. To explore further, turn to **148**.

176

Though you fought as hard as you could, the **Golden Guardian** was too strong for you to defeat. Its heavy blows and metal body proved more than your puny human body could handle and you sink to the floor, succumbing slowly to your injuries. As the light fades from your eyes, the last thing you see is the corridor opening once more, and the Guardian dragging you out.

GAME OVER – BETTER LUCK NEXT TIME!

177

You step close to a nearby pillar and begin to examine it thoroughly. Despite its size and shape, the entire thing seems to be one solid carved object as opposed to several segments fitted together into a single entity – though you have little time to marvel at the architecture that you see before you. An overwhelming sense of dread begins to take hold, rooting you to the spot. It invades your senses, your mind, your very soul, its tendrils grasping at every facet of your being. Even as an eerie blue glow shines at the edge of your vision and something approaches from the direction of the throne, the fear that has taken hold of you keeps you from looking towards it. Only when a heavy blow sends you flying backwards do you manage to come to your senses and face your attacker. As you gaze upon it, you see it is the true form of the thing seated upon the throne: a **Lich**, fully dressed in the clothing of an Incan emperor. you take **9** damage. If you wish to stay and fight, turn to **154**. To run, turn to **150**.

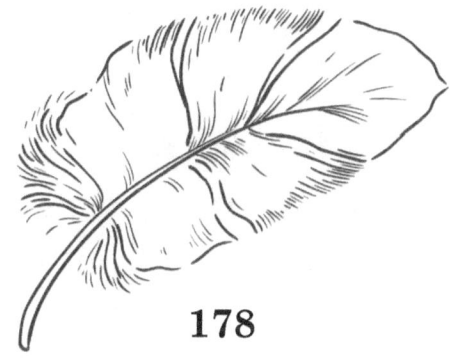

Despite the construct's strength and durability, you prove yourself a worthy match for it, managing to fell the titan. Unable to sustain itself under all the damage it has taken, the **Golden Guardian** freezes, shakes for a few moments then collapses with an almighty crash. There, it lies still, finally having been vanquished − and made safe to examine. As you creep forward and scan your light over the fallen titan's body, you note that without some presumably magic force holding it together, the entire thing has fallen apart into segments. A head, fingers, limbs... all of it has broken off. What's more, further inspection of its body reveals that there is a massive gem hidden inside its head, around the size of an adult human's brain. Just the carat-weight alone is enough to ask a staggering sum at auction, to say nothing of the archaeological and perhaps even scientific value that such a thing might hold.

ITEM AVAILABLE

Golden Guardian Head: The head of a living statue, made almost entirely of gold. Contains a massive gem inside.

Golden Guardian Limbs: The limbs of a living statue, made of gold. Unusually strong, considering the softness of gold.

Golden Guardian Torso: The body of a living statue, made of gold. While it is precious beyond belief, it is immensely large and heavy. Takes up two inventory slots.

Golden Guardian Extremities: The hands and feet of a living statue, composed almost entirely of gold. Weighty, but small enough to stash in your pack.

Having decided which – if any – of these items to bring with you, it's time to search for a way out. Turn to **159**.

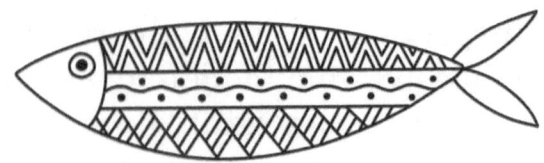

179

A closer inspection of the eagles that have been drawn upon the surface of the throne room's walls reveals little that their smaller predecessors haven't already shown you. Though these are larger, with thicker lines and the presence of gems set deep into them, there is not much difference from the less grandiose versions you have previously examined. As you stand to move onwards however, you find that you are unable to lift yourself off of the ground. Your knees have turned week and your body numb, to the point where even remaining upright is a herculean task. Slowly, the realisation dawns on you that it is fear that roots you to the spot – a sense of all-consuming dread that pervades your entire being. There is nothing that you can do as the faint blue glow in the corner of your eye grows ever more intense, drifting closer from the direction of the throne. You cannot move as it levels a heavy blow against you, sending you crashing back: take **8** damage. The shock of the attack finally sets you free from your self-induced trance. When you finally gaze up to take stock of your attacker, you see what the thing upon the throne truly was. Clad in the clothing of an Incan emperor, the thing that presents itself to you is human only in its shape. It is a **Lich** – an ancient emperor, preserved in undeath. To stand bravely and fight, turn to **154**. If you believe cowardice to be your saviour, turn to **150**.

180

After deliberating between the two options available, you decide to take the southern route. As you make your way along the path, you note that the floor, walls and even ceiling begin to glisten, your footsteps at some point having taking on a slightly wet patter. The noise you yourself are making is, however, drowned out by the cacophony of rushing water in the distance. There can be no doubt that it isn't just drips of water seeping in through the rocks; there must be a significant source nearby for the stone to look like this. To investigate the source of the noise, turn to **117**. Or, if you want to turn back, go to **125**.

181

After carefully estimating the distance and making other such evaluations in your head, you decide to take the plunge and leap forward onto one of the rocks close to the edge of the pit. Fortunately, you make it – though only by about an inch. A slight miscalculation, and you likely would have fallen in, dragged down into the pit's sandy depths. There are still more jumps to go, however. If you decide to grant each one the same mental calculation as the first, turn to **139**. Alternatively, to rush across trusting in your reflexes, turn to **34**.

182

You proceed to follow the path set out for you by the map, whether it takes you across craggy paths lined by rocks threatening to break your bones to splinters, or dense jungle vegetation hiding all manner of deadly plants and vicious predators. It is a tough, unforgiving trek, but eventually you see the path ahead widen and the density of plant life begin to reduce. It seems that there is a clearing up ahead and – if nothing else – it may at least prove a good spot to take a rest while you get your bearings. To take a look at the clearing, turn to **6**.

183

You begin the lengthy process of sorting through the various containers to open and examine in the hopes of finding something that is worth keeping. For the most part though, all you find are the remains of age-old foodstuffs. Some jars contain rotted plant matter that may once have been fruit, fit now only for the insects that scatter at your approach. Others contain a grain of some sort, now more like dust and more likely to poison someone than providing any kind of nutrition. However, amongst the long-since expired produce, something unusual catches your eye – its clean geometrically-cut surfaces make you think it is some kind of key, though it is carved out of stone rather than being made from metal. After you have checked all the containers, you turn your attention towards the stone structure at the room's far end. Taking a close look at the interior, it becomes apparent that it was once used to hold fire – the inside walls are charred, while blackened chunks of kindling lay at the bottom. Whether it was an oven, a furnace, or an elaborate method of sacrificing people to the flame is unclear, as is why it resides in what is ostensibly a storeroom.

ITEM AVAILABLE

Stone Key: A key hidden amongst some grain, carved entirely out of stone.

To return to the corridor, turn to **128**.

184

Before you stands the very temple you have read about so many times – yet no words could ever do its majesty justice. Stone upon stone is piled higher than the eye can see, each block a solid and perfectly-hewn mass that the ravages of time have barely even managed to graze. Intricate carvings run across the base of the temple, only ending when they reach the stairs that reach towards its entrance. After taking a few moments to compose yourself, you make your way to the steps leading up to the entrance. At the top of these stands a stone door, carved with similar patterns to those engraved upon the lowest slabs. It is clear that the door is immensely heavy and would take a vast amount of effort to move even just the amount needed to squeeze yourself through the gap. This would be impossible anyway, as a heavy latch is keeping the door from budging any more than a fraction of an inch in any direction; picking it is likely impossible as you suspect the mechanism would have long since seized shut. You think about the items in your backpack and how you might use them. If you have a **Stick**, turn to **52**. Otherwise, turn to **205**.

185

You begin your trek down the plain corridor to the east, while sweeping your flashlight across the path before you as you walk. Each examination only reveals dirt and dust; in fact, the most interesting thing to see throughout the entire passageway seems to be the tracks left by the droplets of water which made their way to the floor. A ladder leans against a hole in the floor besides a doorway to one side of you, but whatever lays beyond it has been

rendered inaccessible by the walls collapsing in; the hole itself has also long since been filled in. All you can do is continue onwards – turn to **22**.

186

Once more, you emerge into the corridor lined with faded paintings and damaged carvings. Fortunately, there are no undead monstrosities currently seeking to hack you apart, nor cunning traps to help you into an early grave. Relief washes over you as you see what could be an exit at the end of the corridor, signalling the end of your foray into the world of the Inca. You can examine the area further by turning to **43**, or – if you want to leave the temple behind you as quickly as possible – turn to **79** to make your way to the exit.

187

You wander through the maze, searching for any clue that you are taking the right path. The dead end you come across dashes any hope that you are making progress, as does the pile of bones you find there – evidently, you are not the only person to have fallen foul of this maze's clutches. As soon as the floor gives way, you figure out that you have triggered a pressure plate and it dawns on you precisely why so many human remains are in one place; the poison darts now spreading the powerful toxin throughout your body provide adequate explanation. Sadly, it is not a discovery that you will be able to share, as it takes but a few seconds for your body to crumple into a kneeling position on the ground, and less than a minute for you to fall face first into the bone pile, exhaling your final breath.

GAME OVER – BETTER LUCK NEXT TIME!

188

You angle the boat to face down the river, and before it has a chance to get too far away, you jump in and hold on. Considering how light the boat is – and how strong the rapids are – it doesn't take long before you are tossed around like a ragdoll, barely managing to hold on. Every rock and low-hanging lump of wood threatens to tear you apart, and the waters below threaten to drag you to a violent end. You are not dead yet though, and still cling to your craft. Only now do you see properly where the current is taking you – turn to **56**.

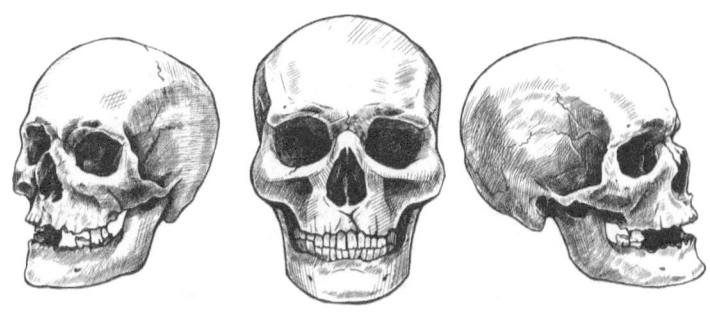

189

Deciding that you would rather brave the strong currents than the flames that appear to boil the water's surface, you leap from the boat, diving down to the riverbed. You avoid the heat successfully and the most that you can feel is a vague warmth from above; the boat itself quickly burns into an unrecognizable mass of ash and charred reeds. Your joy is short-lived, though; your leg catches on a rock beneath the surface, and that single wound is enough to draw the attention of the river's carnivorous predators. The time to make a choice between facing them or the flames is not afforded to you – the underwater denizens choose for you by closing in and devouring your entire body in mere moments.

GAME OVER – BETTER LUCK NEXT TIME!

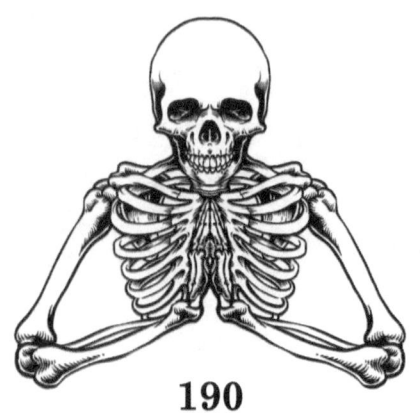

190

You reach out towards the statuette, despite the rising flames surrounding it… but to your surprise, the fire doesn't burn you. It is, instead, pleasantly warm. Unimpeded by the fire, you pull the statuette towards you with one hand, but whilst it does move, it does not come free from the base of the brazier. You quickly deduce that you have, in fact, pulled some kind of lever. What the lever activates becomes apparent just as quickly when the floor beneath you rapidly opens up and you are dumped unceremoniously onto a stone floor below. There is one small stroke of luck in all of this however: the fall was steep enough to kill you instantly, sparing you the agony of a broken spine.

GAME OVER – BETTER LUCK NEXT TIME!

191

You proceed through the doorway; the very second that you are past the threshold, a stone slab covers the exit behind you. It is clear that there is no way back – not without a giant hammer or a box of explosives, neither of which you currently possess. The only way to go is forward – turn to **174**.

192

You step into a brilliantly-lit hall; almost immediately, the glare coming from the room's decorations leave you practically blind. Eventually though, your eyes slowly begin to adjust to the new room's light and you are able to take stock of the scene laid out before you. As with all previous such spaces, the four walls and ceiling are constructed from stone seemingly impervious to anything that could be thrown at it. There is a difference, however. The stone here is in visibly better condition than most of what you have seen before; it's used, of course, but certainly still well- preserved. The floor is largely clear of dirt and the walls remain solid and sturdy. Save for some creeping vines that have somehow rooted themselves in the few cracks in the walls, the room is in fairly good condition. The furniture here is even more surprising; pieces are hewn from stone, woven from wool and cotton, and comprised of wood, and every item you inspect appears almost brand new. To your knowledge, the decor matches known records of the Inca civilisation perfectly – the bed, chairs, tables, and other such things look *almost* as they do in the illustrations you have studied in textbooks – but with one key difference: the gilding. Precious metals accentuate edges, jewels from every stratum of the Earth shine light on intricately-carved details that would take a master craftsman an eternity to create; the room is, simply put, *extravagant*. Evidently, the place seems to be some kind of living quarters; if the decadence all around you is anything to go by, this must have been for someone of extremely high rank. An emperor, perhaps? The legends you are aware of do say that this mythical temple was supposed to house one at some point in history, though with time distorting such tales, it's difficult to know what is true and what is legend. What is important right now is to decide which treasures to take with you.

If you want to examine the wonders of the room right away, turn to **80**. Or, to check the hall through which you came to ensure nothing undead has followed you to this sanctum, turn to **105**.

193

You walk over to the southern door, and begin to inspect it in more detail. However, a closer examination reveals little that you hadn't already discerned with a cursory glance. It is indeed heavy stone, and the gold is – as far as you can tell – genuine. However, what does manage to catch your attention is the sound of footsteps looming over you. Before you have the chance to figure out what is causing them however, something leaps down from above and slaps a weapon against you. Take **5** damage, and turn to **2**.

194

To call the place that you emerge into a *room* is certainly an understatement. To call it a *hall* barely hints at its grandeur. Compared to what has come before, the opulence in front of you sets this area far above anything that lays above or behind it. So incomprehensibly large is the room in which you now find yourself that – whether through time, magic or just man's interference, the tallest trees have managed to sprout up from the floor's stone tiles, reaching high upwards towards the ceiling. The great stone walls are lined both by carvings, and gargantuan pillars. The carvings are of eagles which stand taller than any man, and wider than they are high. Their wings spread out, wholly engulfing anyone who should look upon them; just a glimpse is enough to inspire an overwhelming sense of awe and majesty. Pillars stand to either side of each carving, so far away from where your feet are planted that their tops are shrouded in darkness; so thick are they that to walk around even one feels like it takes an eternity. Each pillar gleams with the now familiar lustre of gold, but within them lay beautiful jewels, a different awe-inspiring pattern of colours and light on every one. Between the pillars and above the carvings, light streams in through square gaps in the walls, though quite where the light is coming from you cannot say. Then there is what lies at the far end. A length of fabric, dyed deep red and hemmed by golden thread, stretches from one end of the floor to the other, leading up to an impressive throne standing proud atop a flight of steps. Rather than being carved from polished stone or crafted by a master woodworker from the most magnificent of trees, this throne is made of metal; lit up by the torches installed to either side, it emits a blinding glare. Although the brightness means you can only catch glimpses from your side-vision, you are absolutely certain that it is made from pure, polished gold. There is something else here, though. You think you can just make out something – or, being logical about this, some*one* upon the throne. Of course, you cannot make out any detail, but you are certain that this thing is human-shaped, though it does not move an inch no matter how long you observe it. Past the throne, you can see the edge of what upon squinting appears to be the frame of a door, though quite where it leads is unclear, and most of it is obscured by the throne itself. It should be, nonetheless, a path forward. As you take your first few steps towards the throne, an earth-shaking clang rings out through the air and the ground beneath you quakes with incredible force. Turning around to check behind you, you are not particularly surprised to see that the entryway has now been blocked off, with no way to open it again. Knowing you must keep your wits about you, you decide to inspect this awesome space further. If you would like to examine the pillars, turn to **177**. If it is the carvings that pique your interest, turn to **179**. If the golden throne deserves your immediate attention, turn to **113**. Or, if you want to make your way to the presumed exit in the southernmost corner, turn to **94**.

195

Slowly, the light grows closer and your trek towards it is thankfully without any pitfalls or poison darts to slow your progress. It still takes longer than you thought, but eventually you manage to make it to the next area in one piece. With bated breath – and with more than a little caution – you step out into a wide-open space. The contrast between the corridor from which you have you emerged and the hall you now behold is enough to give you whiplash. While the path behind you is little more than dust and rock, this giant space is a veritable underground palace, so lavish that it is enough to stop you in your tracks. The walls and the pillars are in nigh-on perfect condition, whether through the dedication of stonemasons fixing even the slightest flaw, or some manner of magic preserving the hall as it must have appeared centuries ago. Even the carvings displayed seem to have been preserved as if they had just been made yesterday. Every inch of the complex and beautiful patterns is inlaid with gold, its glistering shine causing light to bounce off and scatter across the area before it. Even the floor beneath you appears clean and freshly-hewn, with the geometric brickwork showing not even the slightest hint of wear or tear. So great – and perhaps unsettling considering its age – is the majesty of the hall that it takes you a few moments to notice that the space is already generously lit. Torches line the walls, burning with a thick orange light that seems not to fade, no matter how long you observe them for. You click your flashlight off, thinking that you may still need its power at some point in your journey. As you look around more slowly, you notice that the hall appears to hold two paths leading away from the central location. One is to the south, while the other is in the west; both are identical in their construction, however. The doors to these are made of gargantuan blocks of stone and upon each is a carving of an eagle with its wings spread wide, tips almost touching against the entranceway's inner edges. Like the others in this astounding hall, these carvings are inlaid with gold, while the doors themselves are framed by polished, gleaming, golden blocks. If you wish to spend more time examining this space, turn to **14**. If you believe the western door is the path you should first explore, turn to **144**. Or, turn to **193** if the southern route appeals to you most of all.

196

You ready your weapon, and strike it against the door. Despite your blow having no effect other than hurting your hand, a thunderous scraping noise rings out into the air, as if a thousand stones are all grinding against each other. Curious as you are about its source, you are not afforded the chance to investigate as your attempts to force your way in have triggered some kind of trap. You have just enough time to look upwards to note that a huge stone block is descending towards you at breakneck speed... and then blackness.

GAME OVER – BETTER LUCK NEXT TIME!

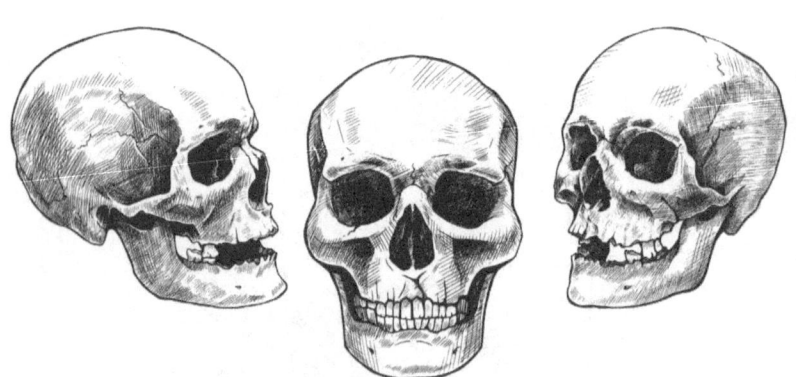

197

After fumbling your way through the murky blackness, there finally seems to be light at the end of the tunnel – quite literally, in this case. A lustrous gleam fills the end of the corridor, acting as a beacon for you to move towards. Still careful to avoid any traps, you tentatively pace towards it. You emerge, and the source of that gleam becomes immediately clear: gold. Mountains upon mountains of glistering gold. It is piled high as far as the eye can see, in blocks, coins and even just raw and unprocessed ore... the entire room is filled to bursting with the precious metal. You wager that there is enough in there to fund a small nation; any treasure hunter with half a brain would kill for the chance to even be given a clue as to its location... and now you can lay claim to this insanely valuable trove spoken of only in myths and legends. Incredibly, the gold is not even the only treasure here. Scattered across the room in heaps are gems of every kind: rubies, sapphires, emeralds, diamonds... whether loose and uncarved, or set into pieces of jewellery that alone would command a king's ransom, they are piled high ready for the taking. So what do you choose?

ITEMS AVAILABLE

Raw Gems: Unprocessed gems of every kind. Some are as small as the tip of your finger, others the size of a fist.

Gold Ore: Unprocessed gold ore. While not as valuable or efficient to carry as processed gold, it is still better than nothing.

Gold Bricks: A set of bricks made from gold. Though heavy, they are quite literally worth their weight in gold, and will fetch a hefty price with the right buyer.

Gold Coins: A collection of loose coins. Likely used more as a tool to barter with European settlers than with the Inca themselves.

Gold Jewellery: Rings, necklaces, bracelets, and other such trinkets – all beset with a litany of jewels. Valuable to collectors and scholars alike, both for their materials and historical value.

Each of these take one slot in your inventory, so fill your boots then turn to **47**.

198

After fishing the blue gem out of your pocket, you hold it against the door, hoping that it will activate some hidden mechanism. The loud rumbling that fills the room after you press it against the middle of the door seems to be promising at first – though not so much when the ground opens up beneath you. As you fall down into the gaping hole revealed by the trapdoor, you barely have enough time to regret your actions before you land unceremoniously on the floor, creating a broken, crumpled and lifeless heap in the bowels of the earth.

GAME OVER – BETTER LUCK NEXT TIME!

199

Despite the sheer number of footsteps thundering towards you, you decide that the best option would be to stand and fight. This quickly turns out to be a terrible – and fatal – decision. Mere moments after the horde emerges into the room, you are reduced to a red mist so quickly that you don't even have time to blink.

GAME OVER – BETTER LUCK NEXT TIME!

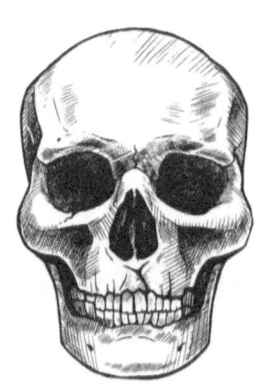

200

Minutes tick by as you tread carefully down the corridor, though your flashlight reveals little of significance, besides your path being on a slight downwards incline. Aside from that, it is all stone, dust and stray vines.

Eventually, after many minutes, the scenery changes, revealing three branching paths, each identical to the others, with darkness too dense for you to see particularly far down them. There appears to be no indication of where to go – until your light catches against a carving on the floor. It is same as those in your notes, pointing you towards one door out of the three. You follow the instructions confidently – turn to **15**.

201

You step back a few metres in preparation of your jump. Then, with every fibre of strength in your body, you dash forward and leap towards a rock you believe to be large enough to land on. You succeed... in a fashion. Though you manage to land on the outcrop, its surface is too flat and slick for you to find any grip, and you slip a split second after making contact. Unable to stop yourself from falling into the torrent below, you have but a brief few moments to contemplate where it all went wrong, before the current shreds you against the jagged stones.

GAME OVER – BETTER LUCK NEXT TIME!

202

The **Lich**'s mastery of the arcane overwhelms you and the last thing you see before the life fades from your body is its staff reaching out towards you, a pale blue light consuming your being. At least, you ponder, there are other souls in this hell to spend eternity with.

GAME OVER – BETTER LUCK NEXT TIME!

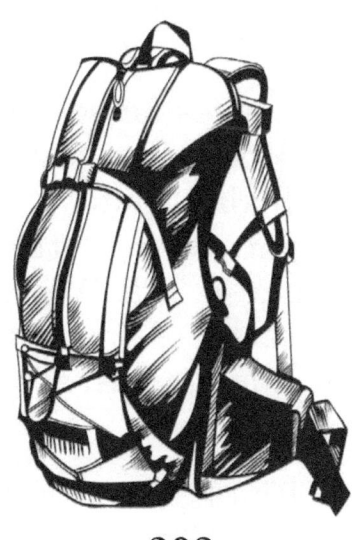

203

After pressing yourself flat against the wall, you begin to shuffle across the ledge. Moving carefully, you do your best to make sure that your weight isn't concentrated too much in any one place and that your balance is kept. Upon reaching the centre however, both ends of the platform begin to fall away, crumbling into chunks which disappear into the sand. Only seconds are left before you yourself will follow them – so a decision must be made, and quickly. To try and leap the large distance to the other side of the pit, turn to **118**. Or, to aim for one of the rocks jutting out of the sand, turn to **115**.

204

You search the shelves for something to help you defeat the incoming horde. The gold is no doubt valuable, but without even a ceremonial weapon amongst the bric-a-brac, you find yourself at a loss. When the undead arrive, you are bereft of anything that could have saved you, and are torn apart before you can even scream.

GAME OVER – BETTER LUCK NEXT TIME!

205

Frustrated by your inability to make it past the temple's heavy door, you trudge angrily back down the steps until you reach the last, on which you sit, huffing to yourself about the difficulties of investigating an ancient temple all by yourself. It takes a while to calm down, but eventually you do. Taking stock of the situation you decide to put some effort into your adventure and jump up with gusto. To take another look around the area, turn to **85**. Alternatively you could climb back up the steps – in which case you should turn to **184**.

206

Congratulations, fearless explorer! You have made it back to London – and what is more, you have some treasure to show for your troubles. It's time to present your loot to the British Museum, who are already tapping up their wealthy backers to ensure they are the ones to put these items on display next to their collection of Egyptian mummies and Elgin marbles. Add up the total value of your plunder from the next page, then read on to see how the chief curator judges you...

ITEM	VALUE
Golden Dagger	£10m
Mysterious Blue Gem	£50m
Statue Gems	£20m
Raw Gems	£175m
Gold Ore	£50m
Gold Bricks	£15m
Gold Coins	£75m
Gold Jewellery	£150m
Golden Guardian Head	£30m
Golden Guardian Limbs	£20m
Golden Guardian Torso	£40m
Golden Guardian Appendages	£150m
Undead Guardian's Spear	£175m
Lich Emperor's Jewellery	£40m
Lich Emperor's Staff	£50m

Comments from the Chief Curator of the British Museum

If you treasure fetches between £0 and £30m

What an utter failure! The costs of the expedition alone must have come to more than the amount your treasure has raised for your family. It seems that the only option is to convince your banker to finance the next adventure... to *Espionage Island!*

If you treasure fetches from £31m to £80m

There are some interesting pieces in the loot you have brought back with you, though there's not really enough here to justify your name being mentioned in the description of the items. Perhaps you should consider going on another treasure hunting trip to solidify your reputation... to find the *Golden Apple!*

If you treasure fetches from £81m to £150m

Well done! Financially, you are definitely set for life, though it seems that it will be the treasures themselves that grab the headlines as opposed to your own name. Money is one thing, but fame? Well, perhaps you should seek out the *Eye of Bain!*

If you treasure fetches from £151m to £300m

What can I say? Oxford University have called to offer you the position of History Professor and an article detailing your exploits is set to appear on page 8 of the *Times*. Oh, is that a little disappointing? Maybe you should take a look into *Ground Zero!*

If you treasure fetches more than £300m

Congratulations! Your story is set to be plastered all over the front pages of every national – and international – newspaper. Your name will go down in history as one of the great explorers, mentioned in the same breath as Ferdinand Magellan, Christopher Columbus and Leif Erikson. You can sit back and relax in your stately mansion, being waited on by your many servants; you'll be completely free of any danger, risk or excitement. Or... you *could* take a look into rumours of... the *Ship of Doom!*

www.ingramcontent.com/pod-product-compliance
Lightning Source LLC
Chambersburg PA
CBHW020958180626
46814CB00003B/1154